SEVERED

DANIEL J. LYONS

Dedicated to my wife and family—your support keeps me going.

PROLOGUE

"It's all fake!" Brian Masters, CEO of Prosperity Portal Systems, shouted as he tossed a portable screen back at his Director of Prosperity Station Security. He turned and stormed out of the room and down the corridor. Myer Giancana, the currently frustrated director, caught the screen after a few fumbles, then followed the CEO.

"This company was built on the slogan 'Live on the stars without compromise'," Masters continued, as he noticed Giancana approaching. "I'm not going to start compromising now."

"Sir, this isn't about compromise, it's about security," Giancana replied, as he caught up with the CEO. "All I'm asking is to publish an alert and authorize some inspections."

"And panic the investors?!" Masters said, sneering, not even glancing back.

"Sir," Giancana struggled to maintain his composure, "investors will be more panicked if anything happens to the station."

"This station has over *fifty thousand* police officers and the Navy's *walking distance* from your office!" Masters' anger propelled him faster down the corridor. "Hell, we even built them custom docking bays to make sure that there would be a scout and a patrol ship here at all times! No third-rate group of *troglodytes* are a threat to this station!"

"Sir, this is not the first credible threat…"

"It's not *credible.*" Masters spun around and thumped a finger into Giancana's chest to enunciate his next few words. "That's my point!"

"Respectfully, sir, all reports indicate that this Reunite Humanity is targeting—"

"Reunite Humanity," Masters scoffed. "Our Portals unite us more than any other point in human history!"

Giancana pressed on with a concerned look. "Sir, there are clear indications that they are attempting to acquire weapons—"

"This station is larger than *any* planetary capital!" Masters replied, his face turning red. "No *protest club* is going to be able to gather enough weapons to do more than embarrass themselves! This matter is *closed*. If you bring it up again, you'd better pack all your *shit* first!"

Masters stormed off.

Giancana closed his eyes for a moment, wiped spittle off his face, then turned and headed back to his office.

Prosperity Station had been constructed using the profits from the corporation's first commercial success—their standardized Door and mount system.

Doors were a personal version of the Portal—a transportation technology that passes an artificial wormhole through an entangled quantum tunnel to allow for instantaneous travel between the two endpoints that make up a full set. The two variations had enabled humanity to fulfill its long-held dream of expanding into the stars.

The station had been carefully positioned close, but not too close, to an unused Portal at the far edge of the poorly regulated H sector.

H sector, known today as the Harvard sector, was the last of the ten First Wave sectors to get up and running, its founding delayed repeatedly by technical failures aboard the automated ship carrying its first Portal. Despite half a century head start, H sector was barely established when the first Second Wave sector was founded.

The early sector government was so eager to recover lost time that they purchased more Portals for internal expansion than they had available settlers.

Taking advantage of their desperation, Prosperity created the concept of a corporate zone, which would have the benefits of a system government, including their own spacecraft registration office, but none of the obligations, like funding Naval ships.

During negotiations, Prosperity agreed to establish a local government on the station in exchange for the zone border being placed just short of the Portal. Since the Portal would be officially located outside the new corporate zone, it would continue to be maintained by the sector government. The maintenance costs, the corporation promised, would be offset by the increased traffic.

The new station was modular in design, with each section complete with its own independent systems. Each module was split into three levels: factory and industrial space at the base, the middle set aside for Prosperity's next big idea, and the top containing a modern city.

After humanity took their Doors into space, the concept of a city changed dramatically. In a reaction to the cramped living conditions on the declining home-world and early expansions within the solar system, very few people actually lived in cities (or at any single location for that matter), preferring to have ample personal space surrounding them. Where older cities had apartments, modern cities had small commuter units, which were often barely larger than the Door mount they were built around. These commuter units eventually became known as Locations and gave a widely spread humanity back a sense of community.

As part of their new station, Prosperity decided to expand on that Location concept and turn their middle decks into what they referred to as a Collection.

These Collection levels were filled with a variety of differently-sized Locations that could meet any budget—from luxury units with actual bedrooms, to tiny, closet-sized units along the outer "cold-wall" of the station. Most Locations fell somewhere in the middle, including a standard Door mount, sockets for communication Conduits (a Prosperity standardization of the original quantum tunnel implementation), and a delivery chute.

Over the centuries, many new modules had been added, and the oldest modules had been replaced, allowing the station to grow to an unprecedented size. The Collection levels of now housed millions of individual Locations, with Doors connecting to every sector of human space.

As the local government was given more authority to foster the appearance of an independent operation, the Prosperity Station Corporate Security office had consequently lost staff and influence. By the time Myer Giancana took over, his position had devolved into little more than a liaison between the corporation, local police, and the Space Defense Alliance Navy.

When Giancana arrived at the security office, he found his second-in-command (and only other member of station corporate security), Jo-anna Henry, standing just inside the door looking concerned.

"Was that as bad as it sounded?" she asked, as Giancana tossed his screen onto his desk. The screen landed hard, slid off the far side, then clattered on the floor.

"Worse," Giancana said, as he angrily pulled out his chair. A loud crunch announced the demise of his much-abused screen. "The man's so pigheaded that he can't, no *won't*, see anything beyond the quarterly balance sheet!" He dropped bonelessly into his chair, ignoring a more subdued selection of crunches.

Henry sat in the guest chair opposite her boss. "Is there anything we can do?"

"Without Master's approval?" Giancana said, in a defeated tone. "Not a thing. The best we can do is stay on our toes and hope whatever's coming will be manageable."

CHAPTER ONE

The quarterback paused, cocked back her arm, and scanned the field while two opposing players converged on her position. Her arm snapped forward, the ball arced towards the end zone, then the screen went blank.

A moment later, "no signal" appeared across the screen beneath an animation of a shrugging squirrel.

"Aaaaug!" Violette Hamilton looked up from where she was sprawled across the sofa. "The feed cut out!"

Across the room, Violette's father, Eric Hamilton, was shaking his screen. "I was in the middle of grocery shopping!"

Both screens flashed red with an incoming override communication from Dianne Hamilton, the captain (also mother and wife respectively) of the PCV *Hamilton* where they resided. "The feeds just went offline, and support is not responding. Can one of you pop through the Door and see what's going on?"

"I'll do it," Violette shouted, as she rushed out of the room. "You know Dad's useless with tech!"

Violette ran into the foyer and, without pausing, punched the Pad on the left side of the Door's frame. The Door blurted a response and, caught by surprise, Violette bounced off the blank and unyielding back of the Door's frame.

"Sagged!" she shouted, pinwheeling her arms in an attempt to recover her balance.

"Language!" her father said, chastising her from just outside the room as she finally crashed to the floor.

"The Door didn't open!" She pointed at it accusingly as her father entered the room.

The Door's frame looked much like an old-fashioned doorframe (although the left side of the frame was much wider to accommodate the control Pad) but without a physical door and with a lightly padded grey panel covering the opening from the back.

The Pad, which Violette hadn't thought to glance at before this point, was currently configured as a raised red triangle on a grey background. Normally the variable surface of the Pad oscillated between two states: a raised blue disk indicating that the Door was open and a green version of the disk that indicated it was closed but ready.

After her father helped her up, Violette flipped out a small panel located just above the Pad—then yelped as a drenk fell out, spread its wings, and flew loudly towards the doorway.

Eric swatted at the insect. It bounced off his fingertips and disappeared into the corridor. "I thought we got rid of those pests!"

They returned their attention to the Door and the status screen built into the back of the newly opened panel.

"Status report," Violette ordered.

The screen lit up. In large white letters on a red background, it displayed:

Portal disabled - Unsafe conditions detected at terminus

Please contact technical support

"Technical support," Violette said.

The Door blurted again, and the message changed to:

Communication failure - Channel sync did not respond

Please contact technical support

"Thanks," she grumbled.

Eric lifted his left arm and tapped a plain black wristband, which chirped softly then projected an image of a middle-aged redheaded woman in the air above his forearm.

"No go here," he told his wife's image. "The Door's fully busted."

Now pacing the room, Violette was aggressively tapping a control panel projected onto her forearm by her own wristband, a two-tone whistle sounding in response to each tap. "I can't get *anything!*"

Violette, suddenly realizing that she was tapping controls like someone her parent's age, quickly moved on to shouting commands at her wrist instead.

Ignoring his daughter, Eric continued. "What if we can't get the Door open?"

A look of concern crossed the image of his wife's face. "I'll be right there."

"Dad, grab a wipe out of the cabinet," Violette said, swiping closed the control panel on her forearm and moving back towards the Door at the back of the narrow foyer. "I want to clean the contacts."

Violette started to release the first of four clamps on the outside corners of the Door, which held it securely in the mounting port built into the wall. As she released the clamp, the status screen went dark and the raised triangle smoothed out, fading to the same grey as the rest of the Pad's surface.

"Help me with this," she said, grabbing her side of the Door.

Her father tucked the container of wipes he just retrieved from a cabinet under his arm, then grabbed the opposite side. After a firm pull, the Door frame came away from the mounting port. They carefully leaned the Door against the cabinets that covered the fore side of the room.

Along the left edge of the newly exposed recession in the wall were two round sockets, a blue one near the midpoint, just behind where the Pad had been, and a red one just above the bottom.

"Here." Her father handed her a moist wipe from the container.

"Thanks." Violette carefully wiped out the blue socket. "Okay, let's put it back."

They both took hold of the Door again, carefully lining up ridges in the mount with matching indents built into the sides of the Door frame. Once it was properly aligned, they pushed hard until there were several loud clicks.

"Let's fasten the clamps and reboot it," Eric said, as he reached up to fasten the top clamp on his side.

After Violette snapped the last clamp back into place, a yellow disk raised up out of the Pad. A moment later, the Door blurted. The disk turned red and reshaped itself into a triangle.

Violette sighed. "Let's try the Conduits and see if we have better luck."

Her father pulled another wipe from the container and joined her at a panel at the midpoint of the aft wall of the room.

The panel contained six sockets arranged in three columns. Populating the left two columns were the family's four Conduits.

The Conduits were six-inch-long cylinders, each containing one end of an entangled quantum tunnel. On the inner end of each conduit was a standardized plug, which had been inserted into the wall panel. Common to each Conduit was a small round data port and a status light, both positioned side-by-side across the middle of their flat outer end. Two of the Conduits in the panel were metallic silver and, along with the single green Conduit, currently displayed red status lights. The final red cylinder's status light was yellow.

The two silver Conduits, both plugged into the center column of sockets, also featured white rectangles on the lower half of the outer end, which had been used to add handwritten labels. The one in the bottom socket was labeled "data," and the one in the top was labeled "system."

The green cylinder, plugged into the lower left-hand socket, was embossed along the top with the two silver overlapping rectangles that formed the Prosperity Portal System's corporate logo and had "SECURE ID P90-00192" engraved along the curving bottom edge.

The red Conduit, in the upper left-hand socket, was the ship's emergency receiver and had no markings.

"Don't touch your mother's," Eric warned, at the sound of his wife's footsteps in the corridor.

"I'm just going to try data," Violette replied, while reaching for the silver Conduit with the corresponding label. She pushed it back into the panel and twisted it counterclockwise. There was a click, and she pulled it out of the panel.

As she removed the Conduit, a green version of the Prosperity logo became visible on the upper side next to a black label reading, "Class A Conduit - Model 439."

She took the wipe from her father and applied it to the contacts on the end of the Conduit, then carefully wiped out one of the previously empty sockets before plugging the Conduit in there—pushing and twisting again until it clicked.

The status light flashed yellow for a moment before changing back to red.

"Nothing," Violette said, disappointed.

A moment later, Dianne Hamilton, dressed in her usual baggy overalls, stepped into the foyer. "Anything?"

"No," her husband replied. "Violette cleaned the contacts on the Door and moved the data Conduit, but neither of them reconnected."

Dianne grunted in response, pulled a worn technician's screen from her pocket, then wiped lint off it with her sleeve.

Glancing at her daughter, she said, "How many times do I have to tell you, cleaning the contacts is an urban myth. Besides, the Door contacts are only for triggering disconnect alarms and uploading to the beacon, they don't affect functionality." She widened her glance to include her husband. "Now, clear a path so I can get a look."

They both stepped aside to allow Dianne to get to the Door. She pulled a cable out of the back of her screen and plugged it into a port in the Door, which had previously been covered by the closed status screen. As she did, the red triangle on the Pad smoothed out and a white numeric keypad rose in its place. She typed in an access code, and the display on her screen changed to show a technician status readout.

"I still don't see any errors on our end," she said, swiping on the screen. "The other side is responding, so the quantum tunnel is fine. Wormhole generator reports ready, backup battery engaged, no network... This can't be right..."

"What?" Violette asked, craning her neck and attempting to read her mother's screen.

"They must be spoofed," Dianne said, with quiet disbelief before continuing in a normal tone. "The sensors read no atmosphere and, frankly an impossible level of radiation. The Door will never engage under these conditions, real or not."

Dianne unplugged the cable and turned to the Conduit panel as Violette shuffled back out of her way.

She plugged the cable into the red Conduit. "The other end of the emergency receiver's on internal power, no transmissions received—nothing that I couldn't see from the bridge." She moved the data Conduit back to its original position. "Since a different socket didn't work, I'm just going to put this back where it belongs."

After the status light illuminated, passing again through flashing yellow to solid red, she plugged in her cable. After a moment, she repeated the process on the other silver Conduit, then finally the green Conduit.

"No local errors or response from any of the remotes," she said, sliding the cable back into her screen. "The power's out."

"Maybe someone broke into our Location and unplugged everything when they spoofed the sensors," Violette suggested.

Her mother rolled her eyes.

Her father looked at her with disbelief. "Who would do that?"

"I can't imagine," her mother answered, not entirely kindly, "but at this point, all we can do is wait for support to respond to the disconnect alarms."

Over an hour later, Violette was angrily pacing again, this time in the Hamilton's family room.

"It *shouldn't* take this long! We should have been up and running in less than half an hour! That's why we paid for the level two support package!"

"*We* paid?" her mother muttered under her breath.

"Even if they smashed everything," Violette said, oblivious to the commentary, "they should have had the tunnels remounted and installed in an alternate Location by now. We should have heard *something!*"

"Well," her father replied, "at least there isn't anything coming through the emergency receiver so it can't be all that serious."

"Unless the station is just gone," Violette grumbled, making an exploding sphere gesture with her hands.

"Don't say that again!" Dianne glared at her daughter with a dark look. "Prosperity is the largest station in the sector. It can't be *just gone!*"

"Then why haven't we heard anything!?" Violette responded in frustration.

"Both of you calm down!" Eric said. "It's probably a big outage, and they just haven't gotten to us yet."

After taking a deep breath Dianne replied, "Your father's right." She forced a weak smile. "Remember when we first moved in and they screwed up our power bill? We were offline for nearly two hours."

Violette's glare was unconvinced.

To prevent his daughter's retort, Eric changed the subject. "Okay, let's watch something and give them time to work. I bet we hear back before it's over."

"Uh, the feeds are down," Violette replied condescendingly. "There's nothing to watch!"

"There's got to be something in the cache." Dianne walked over to the large entertainment screen on the fore wall of the room and plugged her technician's screen into a port on the side. "Here, look, there's plenty of stuff."

The default fine art slideshow faded from the entertainment screen and a list of media options appeared.

"But we've *already* watched those!" Violette shouted in exasperation.

"Pick something that you'd like to watch *again*," her mother responded tersely. "I'm going to lock the cache so that they don't get deleted, just in case."

Violette loudly told the screen, "Weekly Sports Highlights," then grudgingly planted herself on the couch.

CHAPTER TWO

The young couple were lost in each other's eyes as they danced to their favorite piece of classical music, spinning together as the long-dead singer's voice screeched out the catchy refrain.

They were dancing in the middle of a tiled dance floor at the back of a large hall. Ornate columns spaced along the outer walls supported the high arched ceiling and separated large windows that let in the fading sunlight. Several large tables were arranged around the room, along with one smaller table, positioned right near the edge of the dance floor, that had a large tray half full of slices of wedding cake.

The couple's dresses flared as they spun again, his lifting to reveal a large scar on his left calf, which he refused to have nano-scrubbed away and referred to as his "keepsake."

As the oft-repeated story went, eager to impress, he had agreed to join Maria, his current dancing partner, for a day of rock climbing on their first date. Having done very little climbing in the preceding years, he spent nearly a week practicing to make sure he wouldn't embarrass himself.

When the day arrived, he walked to her apartment with great anticipation and complete confidence. That confidence faltered when a step gave way and his foot fell through, a sharp edge opening his calf along the way, until his bodyweight wedged his leg in a hole to just above the knee.

After he was extracted by emergency services, Maria spent the remainder of the day with him in the emergency room. An uncomfortable portion of that time was spent with the skin on his leg held tightly in place by a medical clamp as the skin-join compound stitched the ragged edges back together.

Maria helped him pass the time by maintaining conversations about anything and everything.

Upon his release, they finished the day with a late dinner at his place before she tucked him in for a solid night's rest and kissed him goodnight.

After that day, neither of them had eyes for anyone else.

Other couples danced past, several pausing to congratulate the newlyweds, their voices lost in the pounding music.

The newlyweds paused at the clinking sound of cutlery tapping on wine glasses. They turned to each other just as Captain Alvin Faro's wristband vibrated for his attention.

Reluctantly, he pressed a button on the top of the holographic memory album that sat on the small table just to the left of his command chair. The kissing couple faded, leaving behind a dull, grey-walled room.

The grey room was the bridge of Alvin's ship, the PCV *Faro*, a cargo vessel that had been in his family for three generations. Taking up most of the curved front of the bridge was a large window looking out into space. The squared off back wall was broken only by a single, centrally located arched entryway. His command chair was positioned in the center of the bridge and, aside from the small table, was the only furnishing in the room.

With a sigh, Alvin double tapped his silver wristband, prompting a tall virtual screen to appear in front of him, immediately followed by two curved holographic control surfaces, which grew from either side of the screen and wrapped around Alvin.

The grey of the room faded to black. Beneath the new control panel and the command chair a blue, circular platform with a low silver railing appeared. To Alvin's right, his virtual assistant, currently in the guise of a tall, silver robot, faded into place.

Around the platform, a detailed, but not to scale, view of the space between the vessel's current position and its intended destination began to appear, starting with a large red sphere for their destination, followed by individual stars that appeared in the exact order in which they had been born.

Above his head stretched a thick dotted line that started somewhere behind him and ended at the red sphere in the distance. Each segment of the dotted line had a thinner line extending from its closest edge at a ninety-degree angle, which was surrounded by three figures. The first figure, positioned above the line, was labeled "Time to Destination" and decreased as the lines moved forward, as did the second "Distance to

Destination" number directly below the line. The final figure, positioned off the end of the line, was a countdown clock that indicated when the vessel was expected to reach the start of the connected line segment.

A message appeared on the screen, character by character, as if being typed by hand:

Data feed disconnected - no response from support

The message was redundant, mainly appealing to Alvin's love of turn-of-the-technology dramas and the days of command line computer hacking. A red status indicator on the virtual control surface by his right hand had already provided the same information.

Another red status indicator, labeled **POWER**, had a yellow strip of virtual paper sticking out from its right side reading, in block letters, "Mike – Thursday 8 am" and below that, in handwritten script, "Remember to pay for the parts *before* Wednesday!"

"Jeeves," Alvin said, addressing the robot, "diagnostic report."

A bulky, old-fashioned screen appeared in the robot's right hand. It raised it towards its flat face. A series of whirring noises sounded from inside its holographic arm as it did so.

"My scans indicate that our Location has been compromised." The robot's harsh metallic voice reported, "There is no response from the Conduit, emergency receiver, or Door."

"Check the logs," Alvin commanded, tapping several virtual controls as he cross-checked the robot's findings. "What happened?"

"Searching…" the robot said, its square blue eyes displaying scrolling lines of black pseudo-code. "Just before we lost contact, the Door went into emergency lockdown."

A virtual sheet of red paper suddenly appeared directly in front of Alvin, floating between him and the screen. It was titled "Critical System Failure" and contained a list of warnings:

Primary Zero-Point Generator offline

Secondary Zero-Point Generator operating at 97% capacity

Multiple flares detected - filament failure immanent

Immediate load reduction required

Immediate generator maintenance advised

Alvin flicked the warning away for the thousandth time and asked, "What triggered the lockdown?"

"According to the log," the robot replied, more code scrolling through its eyes, "high radiation levels."

"How is that possible?" Alvin glanced at the robot for the first time.

"Unknown." Its arm emitted more whirring noises as it lowered its screen. "There is no additional data."

"Dismissed," Alvin said with disgust.

The robot faded.

The only reasons that Alvin could come up with to explain why the remote receiver would stop responding so quickly were if it had been tampered with, which he thought highly unlikely, or if it had been completely destroyed, which he thought to be even less likely.

Alvin focused on the virtual control panel in front of him and attempted to connect with the remote end of the emergency receiver, certain that he would have better luck than the virtual robot.

Emergency receivers were part of the legally mandated equipment manifest for any registered spacecraft and were required to operate for at least a year after being disconnected from their normal power source. To achieve this, they were powered by class 5 Zero-Point Generators, which, despite being the smallest and least expensive versions available, made up ninety percent of the cost of the expensive devices.

Although ZPGs were, by far, the safest source of power available, with the damage caused by even the most catastrophic failure being completely contained within the generator's casing, their manufacture was quite the opposite.

The dangerous point occurred during the stage where the Casimir filament aperture was connected between the two ends of the compressed quantum tunnel—a process that was successful only half the time even with modern manufacturing techniques. The danger was in the roughly one-third of these failures that were exothermic.

Although the vast majority of these exothermic failures were fairly minor, ranging from burning out the aperture or quantum tunnel plate to small explosions that destroyed the partially assembled generator, one in ten held the potential for catastrophe. Humanity had learned just how catastrophic in the very early days of human interstellar expansion.

After a failure during early development work aboard Quantum Power Systems' research station in orbit around Mars destroyed a lab and killed several researchers, all ZPG development was moved to the planet Detroit.

Detroit was one of the first planets colonized by humanity and had been wholly funded by private corporations with the intention of establishing a fully industrial planet that would allow for nearly unlimited mining as well as hazardous manufacturing facilities.

Quantum Power Systems set up their new lab on the most remote part of the planet in two parts, positioning the build room and the control room on opposite sides of a mid-sized mountain. Slowly, and after replacing the build room several times, progress was made, and a manufacturing process was established.

The final build room was torn down to make way for a factory so they could move from individual builds to a proper assembly line. The factory included many precautions, including separate and heavily armored rooms where the aperture was to be connected, but the researchers had greatly underestimated the potential yield of a failed connection.

Disaster struck just after the first test run units had been shipped out for review, and the resulting explosion vaporized the mountain and most of the surrounding countryside.

During the literal fallout, the planet's backing corporations collapsed, including Quantum Power Systems.

The explosion was an extinction-level event, with the debris polluting the air and thickening the atmosphere enough to drop temperatures well below the human comfort level. The surviving population had to be evacuated and the planet abandoned.

The test units were positively received and demand for more grew steadily.

Under increasing pressure, the patents and research were finally sold after two decades of legal wrangling. They went to a consortium under the condition that they follow strict guidelines, later incorporated as laws, to prevent future disasters, which limited manufacturing to deep-space stations remotely controlled via secure quantum tunnels.

Due to the costs involved in building these factories, very few ZPGs were manufactured in the early years, mainly large and profitable units destined for military and deep-space use. These costs finally began to fall after Prosperity Portals commercialized a much cheaper generation of secure quantum tunnels, their trademarked Conduit.

After a fourth failed attempt, Alvin finally accepted that the emergency receiver must somehow have been destroyed. It was a hard acceptance because it also meant that his Conduit and Door end points must have met the same fate and that his connection to the rest of humanity was truly severed.

Unless another craft happened to pass the *Faro* in the Prosperity-Ginhard shipping lane, there would be no way to call for help.

Alvin called up the most recent shipping schedule, then closed it quickly after reading that the PCV *Xavier* was not scheduled to depart on its return trip to the station for nearly three months.

The critical system failure warning appeared in front of him again.

He flicked it away and shouted, "Jeeves!" The robot reappeared. "Engage battery power to reduce generator load."

"That is not advised." The robot consulted its screen again. "Battery power is intended for use as an emergency backup."

"This *is* an emergency. Battery power will lower the load on the remaining generator."

"True," the robot was swiping at its screen, "however, severe load reduction would be the most advisable course of action."

"Do both, but maintain full power to any room I'm in."

Looking up from its screen, the robot acquiesced with a nod. "Acknowledged. System power distribution set to follow mode, engaging battery power."

Alvin leaned back in his chair, closed his eyes, and said, "Maria, I have a bad feeling about this."

Several minutes later, he tapped another control to dismiss the robot and virtual controls, levered himself out of his chair, and slowly shuffled out of the room.

His shuffling took him to the midpoint of the *Faro* where the vessel's foyer and cargo elevator were located on opposing sides of the central corridor. Alvin opened a cabinet adjacent to the elevator doors and removed a portable screen containing the current cargo manifest, a small knife, and an extension cord, which he slung over his right shoulder.

Stepping into the elevator car, he tapped the control Pad, which changed from a raised blue down arrow to a raised green square with a recessed down arrow in the center. The rarely-used elevator creaked its way down to the base of the single deck of the attached cargo container.

As the doors rattled open, lights flickered on to reveal long rows of plastic-wrapped pallets containing a variety of packaged Doors ready for market.

Alvin activated the screen, scrolled through the index, then tapped on the "Endpoints" entry.

He groaned as he read the "Y" in the entry's location field. "Of course they're at the back." He made a few more taps on the screen to move the container's starboard cargo arm to the Y section.

Alvin spent several minutes walking down the corridor between the stacked cargo and the cold-wall of the hold, passing through each alphabetical section until he finally reached his destination one section away from the large loading doors. Above his head and nearly to the roof of the container on its main horizontal track awaited the large, articulated cargo arm.

He spent several more minutes leaning against the wall to catch his breath.

The packages on the pallets in the Y section were thinner than the ones in the forward sections and only contained one-half of a Door set with the other half in storage back on Prosperity Station waiting for the new owner to rent a Location on the station to install it in. While both ends of a Door set were technically endpoints, the one containing the emergency beacon was referred to as a terminus and was intended to be installed at the far end of the doorway.

Back to breathing normally, Alvin started to scan the labels on the endpoint packaging, ignoring the white basic configurations as well as a spattering of yellow custom configurations, until he found a pallet filled with packages with the gold labels of deluxe models.

The deluxe models were so named due to containing a class 4 Zero-Point Generator that allowed them to operate without being connected to external power.

Alvin pulled out his screen, called up the cargo arm controls, and entered the pallet number. The arm descended along a vertical track until it reached the first pallet in the stack containing the deluxe Doors. It inserted its cargo forks into the pallet and moved it to an adjacent stack, repeating the process until it reached the requested pallet.

After the cargo arm placed the requested pallet in the corridor, Alvin pulled out his knife and slashed the plastic wrap that held the packaged Doors in place, then pulled out the closet one. After another short rest, he freed the Door from its packaging and leaned it up against the wall.

Despite having an internal power source, the Door endpoint needed to be attached to external power for the initial setup. Alvin grabbed the extension cord, which he had dropped to the floor during his first recovery session, and plugged one end of it into the closest outlet and the other into the lower left-hand corner of the Door.

He flipped out the status screen and pressed the power button on its side, but nothing happened.

After a moment, he cursed himself, then started sorting through the packing materials that he had tossed carelessly aside while freeing the Door. Finally, he found a small box labeled "Mount-free installation kit" and tore it open. Inside the box were two large round plugs, which he left in the box, and four small rectangular plugs, which he removed and inserted into the mount clamp slots at the top and bottom of either side of the outer casing.

He pressed the power button again, and the screen display lit up with:

Auto-configuration in process

A minute later, the screen turned red and displayed:

Terminus not found

Please contact technical support

He tapped on "technical support," and the screen changed to:

Communication failure - Channel sync did not respond

Please contact technical support

Alvin groaned, then started pulling out the next deluxe Door.

After going through every Door on the pallet with the same results, he forced himself to accept that there would be no help coming from the station.

CHAPTER THREE

The PLV *Rockhard* had started out as a municipal passenger shuttle before being retired and sold at auction to, as he loved to remind anyone within earshot, *Captain* Lawrence "Bud" Nesmith. His father had promised him a vessel of his own for his eighteenth birthday, and Captain Bud, as he now preferred to be called, decided that converting the shuttle to his needs would be a fun project.

First, he hired a mechanic to upgrade the shuttle into a long-range vessel suitable for use as an "on the stars" residence. This entailed replacing the original fusion generator with a Zero-Point Generator to eliminate the constant need for refueling. As part of that process the, fuel tanks were removed and the resulting voids converted into storage space.

Next, he brought in a contractor to pull out all the passenger seating and put down flooring to cover the attachment points, remove the larger bathroom with the changing table that he would never need, build an ample bedroom, then upgrade the snack bar and bridge.

Feeling a little left out by this point, and running out of birthday money, Captain Bud decided to finish the last few parts of the job himself. He converted the original data closet into a shower for the adjacent bathroom, relocating the conduit connections into some cabinetry that he acquired for free from a contractor friend, and installed his new Door.

Finally, the *Rockhard* had been registered out of Prosperity Station, and Captain Bud had started his much-anticipated bachelor lifestyle.

Captain Bud was pleased with his latest overnight guest. They had met at a late afternoon "Linner" party thrown by one of his friends. He had been reluctant to attend the party when first invited but, in his typical fashion, he had made the best of it and put his best face forward. His best face had hit it off with a gorgeous woman who had accompanied it, and him, back to the *Rockhard* immediately after the meal.

The *Rockhard*'s bedroom was the largest and most plush space aboard; ornate trim work separated the swirled plasterwork ceiling from the trendy wallpaper, which ended at a highly polished hardwood floor. A series of discrete brass light fixtures were evenly distributed around the ceiling, which, at the onset of the previous evening's activities, had been set to provide minimal illumination. Aside from the bed, there was very little in the room: one nightstand on Captain Bud's side of the bed topped with an antique lamp, a large armoire, and a high-quality materials printer.

Beside the printer stood the sizing rod, a thin, eight-foot-tall sensor that could gather all measurements necessary for the printer to create perfectly tailored clothing—presuming there was enough raw materials in the recycling queue or an equivalent amount of used fabric had been inserted into the direct recycle chute located beneath the print-bed. Despite being capable of printing almost any basic object, as well as simple machines, like an adjustable spanner, Captain Bud utilized it exclusively to print out the fashions that were required to maintain his social standing.

He rolled out of bed with practiced caution, making sure that he didn't disturb whatever her name was.

Before leaving the room, he spent a long moment appreciating the view of her muscular leg sticking out from beneath the twisted silk sheets of his emperor-sized bed.

Finally, sighing with contentment and scratching his privates, he turned, left the room, and crossed the *Rockhard*'s central corridor to the small bathroom. After closing and locking the door behind him, he stepped into the even smaller, and not quite square, shower to start his daily grooming routine.

An hour later, he reluctantly stopped primping his spiky hair to answer a loud call at the door.

"I'm due at work in twenty and your Door won't open!" a female voice shouted. "I can't even connect to your feed!"

"Chill," he said confidently, as he opened the door, "the *Captain* is on deck."

Wrapped in nothing but a towel, he strutted past her and into the main living area of the vessel.

This living area was the second largest space on board and was open to the *Rockhard*'s central corridor. It was split into two undivided areas according to flooring type: carpeted on the aft end and tiled on the fore.

The tiled half of the room contained a battered dining table and three mismatched chairs. Past the forward wall was the kitchen, accessible through a squared off entryway and a large serving window with a small shelf beneath it.

The Door was located in the carpeted section, squeezed between the aft wall (which was covered by an irregular collection of cabinets, drawers, and open nooks) and a large top-of-the-line entertainment screen. All the nooks in the aft wall contained framed screens displaying Captain Bud participating in, what he felt to be, an impressive variety of activities.

Opposite the entertainment screen, with the two legs placed just past the raised edge of the carpet to give it a slight backwards tilt, was an ancient and heavily patched red couch.

Captain Bud approached the Door; it was attached to the cold-wall of the room by four short lengths of grey tubing. One end of each tube was flattened and inserted into a mounting clamp slot in the Door's frame while the other end was embedded into a small grey blob stuck to the wall. Two ratty cables snaked from behind the Door frame and out of the room through a roughly cut hole.

"Where did you get this thing anyway?" She gestured towards the Door. "I've never even heard of Archer Engineering."

"They mainly make industrial screens. A good friend of mine works for them and got me an amazing deal." He toggled the open switch a few times, *hmm'd* thoughtfully, then said, "I've never had any problems with it before. I'll run some diagnostics from the bridge."

Captain Bud left the room, slightly quicker than would seem necessary, and headed towards the front end of the corridor. She followed but was brought up short when he shut and locked the door behind him.

She sighed, "I'm *so* gonna be late."

Twenty minutes later, still wearing just the towel, Captain Bud returned from the bridge.

"Okay, the skinny is that there's some sort of communications disruption. I've set course for the station at top speed, *just as a precaution*, but I'm sure we'll be reconnected long before we arrive." At her concerned look, he added, "There's nothing to worry about."

"Nothing to worry about?" she said angrily. "I've got a *job* to get to!"

"Now you have a *vacation* to get to!" he retorted with a wide grin. "*With the Captain!*"

"I don't think that's quite the treat you imagine it is," she replied coldly.

"You're such a kidder," Captain Bud said, with a dismissive gesture and a laugh.

"I'll *kid* you if you don't start taking this seriously!" She balled her hands into fists as she shouted, "What kind of *disruption* blocks Doors *and* Conduits? What *the hell* is going on?!"

"C'mon, Aria, *chill!*" Captain Bud said, with a hurt expression as he started to make his way towards the bedroom.

"Ariel, it's *Ariel,*" she responded, in an even colder tone.

"Uh, meant like a nickname," Captain Bud attempted, while paused in the bedroom doorway.

"I'm not big on *nicknames,*" she snarled back, "so stick with Ariel."

"Sure, we're chill!" He closed the bedroom door behind him.

She rolled her eyes, sat down on the couch, and addressed her red wristband, which was coordinated with her now rumpled party attire. "List all local content."

A display was projected above her forearm with a disappointingly short list of items.

"Bring up tomorrow's presentation." At her command, the screen moved farther away and expanded. "Let's start on page six. I wasn't happy with that anyways."

Over an hour later, Captain Bud stepped out of the bedroom.

Ariel looked up. "Reconnected yet?"

"No, I don't think so," he replied, pulling at his shirt in discomfort.

"Maybe you should *actually check.*"

"Sure, sure," Captain Bud said, turning towards the bridge. "That's what I was *going* to do."

Ariel grunted and turned back to her presentation. "Next page."

Captain Bud returned a few minutes later. "Nothing yet, but I set the diagnostic scan to run continuously, so we'll know immediately when they get everything back to normal."

"And how long are we going to be stranded out here?"

"Stranded is hardly fair," Captain Bud said, with a theatrical hurt expression. "I'm sure we'll be connected again before we know it."

"Okay," Ariel said struggling to keep her voice calm. "What's our ETA to the station?"

"Not long."

Ariel gave him a dark look that had little effect.

"Only a couple of weeks *at the most.*"

Ariel looked disappointed for a moment before returning to her presentation.

"Ooh," Captain Bud said, to dispel the quiet, "is that for work? You never told me what you do for a living."

"I'm a sales associate for Prosperity," Ariel said woodenly, before continuing in an annoyed tone. "At least I *was* back when I was actually *showing up for work.*"

"I'm sure you'll be there by lunch," he said with a grin. "What does a 'sales associate' do anyways?"

Ariel gave him a hard stare. "I convince people to buy things from us that they were planning to purchase from someone else."

"Cool, cool. How long have you been doing it?"

"An hour less than I was *supposed* to be doing it."

After a few seconds of silence, Captain Bud's face lit up, and he opened his mouth. At her angry look, the unexpressed thought retreated to the far side of his brain and hid quite effectively.

"Uh," he started, searching for a replacement thought, "I should probably conduct my daily inspection."

Captain Bud jumped up and fled to the back of the ship, where he let himself into the airlock for the docking hatch.

After ten minutes of looking out the small, round window in the center of the hatch, he returned and, with exaggerated casualness, walked to the bridge.

An hour later, Captain Bud finished his "inspection" and started pacing back and forth along the corridor.

"I usually break for lunch around now," Ariel said from the couch where she had spent nearly the entire morning. "Do you have anything to eat around here?"

"Lots!" Captain Bud jumped up from the best of the three dining room chairs (the blue one with the ample padding) where he had finally settled. "I'll grab some meal kits from the kitchen."

"Meal kits? Aren't those *way* more expensive than just using regular cartridges?"

"Not if you know where to buy them," Captain Bud replied, as he opened a cabinet attached to the cold-wall of the kitchen. "Besides, it's *so* much easier—one cartridge and you're done!"

The inside of the cabinet had no shelves and contained four brown boxes, along with a haphazard selection of loose meal kit cartridges.

"*Four* cases of chili fries?!" Ariel said, after reading the red labels stuck to the sides of the brown boxes.

"Got them on clearance after they changed the potato recipe," Captain Bud said proudly. Then, looking suddenly uncomfortable, he added, "There's some burgers and fish and chips in here, too." He pulled out two appropriately labeled kits to illustrate his point.

"It doesn't look like there's enough in here to last all that long."

"Don't worry," he replied with confidence. "There's plenty more below deck."

"Oh, then I'll just go see if there's anything more to my liking down there. Or maybe I can make something good out of the emergency supplies…"

"Not necessary!" Captain Bud said quickly. "Besides, it's just an unfinished half-deck crawlspace, totally unsuitable for guests. And, as your host, *I* should be serving *you!*" At her incredulous look, he added, "If it will make you feel better, I'll go below, pick up a better variety of kits, and double-check the rest of the supplies."

"It would make me feel *much* better," Ariel said ingenuously, grabbing the burger kit cartridge from Captain Bud's hand and roughly tearing off the seal.

"Sure, sure." Captain Bud placed the fish and chips cartridge down on the counter and started through the corridor entryway. "Make your lunch while I check the supplies. But, starting tonight, I'm *Chef* Bud!"

Ariel groaned, then focused on inserting the pre-programmed cartridge into the kitchen printer.

"Plates are in the cabinet just above the printer," Captain Bud said, with a sense of relief before heading towards the bridge where the hatch to the utility and storage deck was located.

He returned a short while later with two boxes full of cartridges, mostly burgers but also including more fish and chips, as well as a variety of pasta and noodle dishes.

After a painfully long afternoon, broken up by two more failed attempts by Captain Bud to strike up conversations with his unhappy companion and a catered kit dinner of fish and chips (with a side of chili fries), the day finally came to a welcome close.

"It's late, let's turn in." Captain Bud smiled suggestively.

"I'm *so* ready to turn in." Ariel got up quickly and moved across to the bedroom doorway. "But, one thing's for sure." She stepped back into the room and slapped the Pad beside the door. "You're sleeping on the couch, *Captain!*"

The door shut and locked with a loud, simulated click.

Chapter Four

The Hamilton family was gathered in their dining room and had just pushed their dirty breakfast dishes into the middle of the square table.

"Okay," Dianne started from her side of the table, "I literally cannot conceive of a situation where control would let this much time pass without either broadcasting some kind of message or restoring power. Even if it was just our Location, and support somehow missed the disconnect alarm, the disruption in my secure feed would have brought corporate security running by now just in case a rival was trying to steal this week's timesheets."

The attempt at humor fell flat. She cleared her throat and continued with determination.

"I've decided that we need to make a plan," she said. "We're scheduled to arrive in Ginhard in a little over a year, but without being able to resupply from the station, we'll have to find a way to get there sooner. I ran the numbers and think that we can cut travel time down to around six months."

"Six months!" Violette shouted. "We can't be alone for *six months!*"

"Violette!" her mother shouted back, "just listen!"

"But what about the cargo?" Violette insisted loudly, standing up so quickly that her chair toppled over behind her. "There must be a Door we could borrow?"

"Violette, please…" her father started.

"No," her mother cut in sharply. "I checked. We're carrying full sets, no endpoints. We need to make port, and there's nothing closer than Ginhard, so that's our only option until and unless we get reconnected."

"Fine, then push the max button and let's go," Violette said sulkily, while righting her chair.

"We can't just 'push the max button.'" Dianne glanced at her husband for support. He smiled weakly in response. "Our power distributers need replacing before we could even try to reach max."

"Didn't Mike say it would only take a couple of hours when he dropped off the parts?" Eric asked.

"Yes, but Mike's not going to be able to take care of it for us." Dianne paused to collect her thoughts. "In theory, it should be straightforward; we just follow the instructions to swap out the parts. But Mike also said that it would be a two-person job, so I'd like both of you to help.

"The other big issue," Dianne continued, after her family agreed to her request, "is food. We need to figure out what we have and how to make it last until we get to port. The command system came with a voyage planner app. We've never used it, but if we enter everything we have on board, it should be able to use the flight plan that I just updated to work out a meal plan. Eric, I need you and Violette to inventory everything in the kitchen and pantry, including the emergency supplies. I'm going to go through the storeroom, find the new distributers, and see if there's anything else in there that we can use."

Even after the lights flickered on, the storeroom was dark and, despite its size, claustrophobic. Three dusty bicycles rested on wall mounts just beyond the light switch to the left of the still open double door.

On the other side of the door was the family's materials printer, configured for storage, with its clamshell top closed tightly over its large print-bed, and its sizing rod tucked close against its right side.

A variety of differently shaped and colored containers were strapped in awkward bundles along both side walls. Other piles of detritus filled several large bins, each with an attached fabric web cover—only one of which was actually securing the bin's contents. Each bin sat atop a short pedestal that was mounted to connection points built into the floor. Some of them were nearly touching while others sat in isolation. The only regularity to their arrangement was a wide passageway through the middle of the room that led to a second set of double doors at the back.

Dianne approached the nearest bin and glanced from her screen to the contents. "So, according to the inventory, this should be planet-side clothing." She pushed aside a broken screen to reveal one glove and a box full of wires. She continued shuffling through the contents, moving aside two cooking pots, one of which showed clear signs of scorching; a torn sweater; and a box marked "Kitchen utensils," containing a collection of Violette's old toys.

"I'm never letting them in here again."

Eric and Violette walked through the kitchen and stopped at the pantry entrance.

"Okay…" Eric said, looking into the room.

With the sole exception of the space above and immediately beside the entrance, every wall in the pantry was covered by floor to ceiling shelving, with a narrow aisle to either side of the doorway providing access. The shelves were filled with a variety of boxes and containers, which grew more and more dusty the farther they were from the door.

"How do we want to handle this?" he asked.

Wrinkling her nose at some of the dustier containers, Violette said, "I think it would be easier if we moved everything into the kitchen so we can get it organized and cleaned before we put it back."

"Good thought," Eric replied, tapping on the screen he was carrying. "I'll load up the app on the screen in the kitchen, and we can get started."

As he tapped, a blue window appeared on the kitchen screen (which was positioned just above the largest counter immediately forward of the sink) titled "Scan Supplies," with a block of instructions in smaller print. A previously undistinguished section of the screen's frame, just to the left of the stylized "PY" of the Panomy logo, lit up as the scanner engaged.

Reading the instructions, Eric said, "It looks like we can scan full, sealed packages but will have to log partial packages manually."

"A complete inventory," Violette said, grinning. "That will make Mom *so* happy!"

"Hush, and be *helpful* for a change," her father teased, as he tossed his screen onto the kitchen counter.

"I can't even remember the last time we used the kitchen printer," Eric said a short while later, as he retrieved a box labeled "Wheat Cereal Cartridges (24 count)."

"Because it sucks!" Violette said, as she placed the containers of tomato puree that she was carrying onto a stack of identical containers in the kitchen.

"It does not." He paused to consider. "You just have to stick to untextured food."

"Who eats *untextured* food?" Violette asked as she stepped into the pantry to take the box of cartridges from her father.

"You used to love the banana pudding." Her father stacked a second identical box on top of the first.

"I used to love sucking my toes, too," she said, as she turned towards the kitchen and started grinning to herself, "but I gave that up *after* the last time we printed dinner!"

Eric chuckled as he slid a third box of cartridges, powdered protein this time, out from the very back of the shelf. "You're never going to let us live that photo down, are you?"

"You can't show baby photos to boyfriends!" she said, laughing. "It's Parenting 101!"

He chuckled again in response as he started to pull one of the dustier boxes from the far corner on the cold-wall side of the room. It resisted for a moment, then came free with a ripping sound.

"Something smells," Violette said, stepping up behind him and scrunching up her nose.

"Yeah, these boxes haven't been touched in a while." Eric examined the dusty box in his hands. It had been sitting on its side in a puddle of some dark, now hardened, substance, which had captured most of the thin plastic label that described the contents of the box. "You'll have to open this one to figure out what's inside."

As they moved through the increasingly dusty boxes, the smell grew stronger.

"Something moved!" Violette shrieked.

"Where?" Eric asked, setting the box he just picked up down on an empty shelf.

"It came from behind that next box of cartridges!" Violette said.

Eric cautiously slid the indicated box to the edge of the shelf. Several insects skittered out from behind it and disappeared through a gap between the shelf and the wall.

"I found the smell, and where the drenks were coming from," he said, as more insects fled for the gap. "Quick, get a plastic bag from the kitchen."

Violette ran into the kitchen and started opening and closing drawers.

Her father sighed. "The bottom drawer to the right of the sink."

"Oh, yeah," Violette's voice replied. "Got it!"

She rushed back, shaking the bag open along the way.

"Hold it open as wide as you can," Eric said, while taking hold of the infested box.

She did, and Eric quickly moved the box from the shelf, spinning it in mid-air to move a newly discovered hole so that it pointed up in an attempt to slow the stream of escaping insects.

He dropped the box into the bag, then started it spinning to create a twisted neck. "Hold it closed so none of them get out! I'm going to see if there are any more."

"Hurry," she said, nervously dancing in place. "This is *so* gross! I *sleep* on the other side of that wall!"

Eric glanced back into the dusty shelf and saw that the newly exposed boxes were discolored and swarming with drenks.

"Oh, frag," he cursed. "We're going to need more bags."

As the final squirming bag was inserted into the recycling chute, Violette's face, which had maintained a disgusted and put-upon look since the first, suddenly brightened. "I just remembered something!"

"What?" her father asked in confusion, as she rushed from the room.

"The shuttle!" her voice replied from the corridor. "Be right back!"

Violette passed her bedroom, then rounded the corner into the corridor that separated the bridge from the rest of the ship. The short corridor ended at a stairwell, which she ran down two steps at a time, skidding across the landing at the half level and continuing down to the shuttle deck.

She punched a Pad beside the heavy pressure doors at the bottom of the stairs. The raised disk changed from blue to green, then the doors slid apart.

The shuttle bay was cold and contained the back half of the Hamilton family's rarely used short-range shuttle. The other half of the shuttle was on the opposite side of a pressure curtain that both held it in place and retained the room's atmosphere. The shuttle was sitting on the port side of the room, which allowed for a loading area on the other side that had easy access to an elevator located in the aft-starboard corner of the room.

Violette approached the shuttle's hatch, which spanned half of the visible starboard side of the shuttle, and punched the Pad just to the left of it. When the pad finished changing from a red padlock shape to a pulsing blue circle, she said, "Open sesame!"

"Voiceprint accepted," the shuttle replied, as the hatch pushed outward then split down the middle. The two panels slid apart along the side of the shuttle's hull until they cleared the hatchway and moved slightly inward to lock into place.

Violette eagerly rushed inside.

The shuttle had always been Violette's safe place, a retreat where she could work through her feelings during those times when she was unable to get off the ship due to the hour or periodic groundings. She had many happy memories of sitting in the command chair watching the stars and had once spent hours going through every nook and cranny of the shuttle after a terrible fight with her father. Usually, just being in the shuttle calmed her down, but today she felt uneasy.

After a moment attempting to decipher her unease, she shook her head and moved towards the back of the shuttle. She stopped at a set of cabinets just opposite the two bunks folded up against the wall. She pulled open the bottom-most cabinet, the inside of which was painted red, and grabbed a large yellow bag from a shelf labeled "Survival Kit" in white block letters. She pulled apart the Velcro closure and started fishing around inside, periodically removing hard grey, sealed plastic boxes.

The first box was labeled "spaghetti and sauce," the second and third, "beef stroganoff," and the fourth, "shrimp and grits." After removing three dozen of the boxes, including ten smaller boxes with labels like "apple crisp" and "peach cobbler," she pulled out a yellow satchel and stuffed them all inside.

Smiling, she hefted the supplies over her right shoulder and exited the shuttle.

Later, upon returning to the dining room, Eric placed his screen on the table beside his already seated wife.

"Good news. The app says that we'll make it to port," he said, as he sat down.

"Bad news," he continued, as Violette sat down beside him. "The emergency supplies were all expired—some literally by years."

"And full of drenks," Violette elaborated.

"Fortunately," her father added, slightly louder than necessary, "most of the base protein and some of the cereal cartridges survived and should still be edible. We'll have to put up with a lot of smaller portions and *way* too many protein bars, but we'll make it."

"Tell her about the shuttle!" Violette interjected.

"Okay, okay," he replied, as her mother sighed. "Violette pulled the survival kit from the shuttle, which gives us both another couple of weeks of meals and a little bit of variety. Everything is past the 'best by' date, but it's mostly freeze-dried, so we're not worried."

"And Dad's looking forward to printing out some *untextured* food for breakfast in the morning!" Violette volunteered happily.

Dianne looked at her in confusion.

"I'll explain later," Eric said to his wife, then addressed his daughter. "We'll be happy we have the printer by the end of this."

"We'd be *even happier* if we had upgraded to a better model," Violette responded, "like I've wanted to do *for years.*"

"I doubt that the gourmet model you wanted would be able to make anything different with the cartridges we have left," Dianne said.

"Yeah, okay," Violette agreed grudgingly, "but I bet we would have kept better track of those cartridges if we had a printer that actually printed something *edible!*"

"Beside the point," Eric said.

"I found the parts," Dianne quickly interjected, to prevent Violette's response. She gestured towards two blue plastic boxes sitting on the table beside her. "Which is surprising considering the mess in there, but nothing else that would be of any use. I also ran a systems check; we're fine for air, power, and water. None of our filters are more than a few months old, and there wasn't a single error on any of the Zero-Point Generators—not even the class 3 in the hold, which I'm pretty sure is older than all of us put together."

"So, can we start the repairs now?" Violette asked. "The faster we get going the better!"

"No," her mother replied. "I don't know how long it will take and don't want to take the chance of having the engines down all night. We'll get a good night's sleep and swap out the distributers after breakfast."

CHAPTER FIVE

"Well, Maria," Alvin Faro said, as he stepped into the dining room of the PCV *Faro*, "we're another day closer."

The *Faro*'s dining room was luxurious—centered around a large mahogany table with eight matching chairs, all shining and scratch-free despite their age. The set had belonged to Alvin's grandfather and he had very fond memories working together with his father to repair every scratch or ding that they picked up.

Above the table, a crystal chandelier that had also dated from his grandfather's time, hung from a mount that replaced one of the light panels, which covered the rest of the ceiling.

Alvin pulled the last piece of fruit out of a wooden bowl on the kitchen end of the table. "Do you mind?"

At the lack of reply, he took a big bite, savoring the green apple's tart flavor.

"You're too good to me. Let's see what we can make for dinner."

He moved on into the kitchen and, after finishing his apple, started pulling cartridges from a cabinet above the well-worn printer.

The printer was a high-end model, an indulgence that had started with an overly generous wedding present from a wealthy friend. Having lived the majority of his life on the *Faro* with his father and a printer that only just met the SDA shipping code's legal requirements for printing out emergency supplies, the printer's output had been a new experience for Alvin.

With multiple variable-temperature printheads, it was able to create complex meals in a single pass, unlike the fixed room temperature, hot and cold nozzles on the single printhead found in the basic models that he had grown up with. And, with the built-in dinnerware printhead and attached utensil printer, everything necessary for a meal for them both could be printed simultaneously.

He and Maria had quickly gotten accustomed to the, as the packaging stated, "chef-quality" food that it produced and had replaced it with a similar model when it started to break down.

He finished inserting the last of the cartridges, one labeled pastry, closed the cover, then shouted, "Jeeves!"

The silver robot appeared in the kitchen beside him, its head held at an inquisitive angle.

"We're having beef Wellington tonight."

The robot's ancient screen appeared in its hand. It lifted it with the usual whirring, then tapped on it several times. "Program loaded. Your meal will be ready in three minutes."

"Thank you, Jeeves. Activate date night before you go."

The robot started tapping.

In the dining room, the lights in the chandelier came on, and the ceiling panels went dark.

In the kitchen, Jeeves faded.

"Food in five," Alvin called loudly. "Can you set the table?"

Five minutes later, after Alvin had collected a fork and knife from the utensils printer and placed them on the side of his steaming plate of food, he lifted the plate in one hand and his drink in the other, then headed into the dining room.

"The last beef cartridge is getting low," he said, as he settled at the table, "but I think we can squeeze one more meal out of it. I told you we should have stocked up last time we ordered groceries."

He smiled to take the edge off his comment, as he carefully positioned his utensils on either side of his plate.

"I'm looking forward to this. It's been a while since we had Wellington."

After dinner, Alvin dropped his knife, fork, and thoroughly cleared plate into the kitchen recycling chute and headed to the bridge.

Once in his command chair and surrounded by the virtual control room, he summoned his virtual assistant again and started his increasingly uncomfortable end-of-day routine.

"Any contacts?"

"Negative," the robot replied. "No other craft detected."

With his usual hopeless feeling, Alvin asked, "And the Conduit?"

"Still unresponsive."

Alvin decided to try something different. "Are there any references to similar outages lasting this long?"

"Not within the local database."

"Any ideas?"

Glancing at Alvin with a nearly palpable look of dismay, Jeeves replied, "This unit is not programmed for independent thought."

"Of course not," Alvin mumbled, closing his eyes and leaning back.

After a few minutes, and with resignation, he tapped a control and the virtual control room gave way to grey reality.

He stood slowly and headed towards bed.

On his way, Alvin passed by the bedroom and continued on to the utility room just past the cargo elevator at the middle of the vessel. When he arrived, he tapped a pre-programmed button on the printer to make up a new pair of pajamas. He put them on as soon as they were ready, enjoying the warm feel of the freshly-printed fabric against his skin.

He felt himself relax slightly as he stepped into the bedroom and was greeted by the tranquil oceanfront view.

The decor of the bedroom had been Maria's idea and reflected her life-long nostalgia for the great outdoors. The oceanfront and beach were projected on the cold-wall of the room, with the sand extending a short distance inwards before transitioning into the grass-covered clearing that the bed and other furniture sat upon. Behind Alvin was a thick forest, an image partially spoiled by the, now nearly closed, bedroom door. Above his head was a clear, starry night sky which was, supposedly, an actual scan of Earth's sky illicitly taken right under the noses of the Firm Standing families who now ruled the planet as their own private sanctum.

Firm Standing was a label that they had coined themselves in order to glorify their ancestry and reinforce the official line that only their families had possessed the will and foresight to remain on Earth while the rest of humanity fled.

Despite the insistence of their official history, none of the Firm Standing families maintained more than token residences on the planet during its darkest, and most polluted, years—those centered around The Flight to Save Humanity.

The Flight to Save Humanity started out with a series of automated spacecraft powered by the first generation of faster-than-light drives, which lowered interstellar travel time to mere decades, and were filled with hibernating colonists. Despite the great optimism that surrounded their launch, and the hard work of thousands of technicians monitoring the voyages, few ever reached their destinations.

After the invention of the Portal, which captured humanity's imagination with the promise of instant interstellar travel, a second phase was planned. This phase would formally establish twelve sectors extending out around Earth along the galactic plane. Each sector would be centered around a Portal endpoint, with the other located in high orbit around Earth. The plan called for these Portals to be delivered by, as the promoters were always quick to add, greatly improved automated spacecraft programmed to configure and deploy the power-hungry devices upon arrival.

Due to manufacturing delays that stretched long past the "less than two years" estimate, the plan was scaled back to ten sectors, one for each of the Portal sets successfully constructed after five years. The Earth governments, frustrated by the delays and the lost years of emigration, insisted that the Portals be repositioned to Mars orbit, "to allow Earth space to heal."

In a continuation of the adversity that plagued humanity's early interstellar expansion, only six of the Portals arrived on schedule. The last four had to be recovered by manned expeditions, which then had to escort the Portals for the remainder of their voyages. These final four sectors never recovered from that delayed start and are still considered to be backwaters of little import.

Fifty years later, the First Wave Coalition—which linked the first ten sectors together, along with the Sol system government that was formed as Earth's influence and interest in the rest of the system waned—planned a Second Wave of Human Expansion. With this new terminology featuring heavily in their marketing efforts, the latter half of the Flight became retroactively known as the First Wave of Human Expansion. The terminology stuck and was used again for the third, and final, wave a century later.

Also omitted from the official histories was the fact the Firm Standing families had surreptitiously taken over nearly all of Earth's failing countries and used that influence to encourage "the dregs of humanity" to depart Earth for space. Officially speaking, their ownership didn't start until several years after the First Wave when it was "happily" accepted by the old governments as the necessary first step towards recovering humanity's soiled home-world.

The *Faro*'s marital bed had been constructed from simulated rough-cut logs, with larger trunks along the base and at the four corners and smaller ones filling in the arching head and footboards.

The nightstands and closets were of a similarly rustic design and had been handcrafted as wedding presents from Maria's favorite uncle.

Alvin slid beneath the covers on his side of the bed and, with a deep sigh and great sadness, said, "Maria, it's been a week, and I don't think I can last too much longer out here all alone."

He slid his hand over to the empty side of the bed where, until six weeks ago, his late wife had slept. He crumpled the under-sheet in his fist and cried himself to sleep, just as he had every night since contact with the station, and his few remaining friends, had ended.

Alvin woke up the next morning and, with a new resolve, headed directly to the bridge. He didn't even take the time to change out of his new pajamas, which were now heavily rumpled after a night of troubled tossing and turning.

"Jeeves!" Alvin shouted unnecessarily, as the virtual control room started to appear around him.

The silver robot stepped into being, its hands folded in front of it in supplication.

"Set engines to maximum," Alvin said firmly.

"That is not advisable, sir." The robot consulted its screen. "With the current condition of the remaining generator and rapidly depleting battery levels, a catastrophic and unrecoverable system failure is extremely likely. Reduction in speed and power load is strongly recommended."

Alvin took a deep breath, having already decided that the risk was preferable to the solitude. "Override safety protocols and execute my order."

The robot's eyes turned red. It nodded and replied, "Engines set to maximum, ETA to Ginhard twenty-three days."

CHAPTER SIX

Ariel awoke dreading yet another day aboard the PLV *Rockhard*. It had been a frustrating night on the couch filled with angry dreams after she'd lost the nightly power struggle over the bedroom.

"Is that you?" Captain Bud's voice asked from the kitchen.

"As opposed to?" she replied unkindly.

"I'll print you something for breakfast," he said flatly, over the sounds of a meal kit cartridge being inserted into the printer.

Ariel sat down at the table for what she expected to be a completely unsatisfying meal.

"I still can't connect to anything," she said, as Captain Bud exited the kitchen with two glasses of water, one of which he placed in front of her.

"No changes reported by the diagnostics yet," he answered, in what he expected to be a confident and reassuring tone, "but we're another day closer to the station."

"I think it's time to start broadcasting an SOS," Ariel said with conviction.

"Not this *again!*" Captain Bud struggled to hide his annoyance. "Sending an SOS requires a *documented* emergency. *This* is a minor inconvenience at most."

"Have you *ever* been disconnected this long?"

"Once," he said with discomfort, "during a bit of a billing dispute..."

"And under *normal* circumstances?"

"No."

"Then this sounds like an emergency to me."

"Alita, chill..." Captain Bud said, trying to sound soothing.

"*Ariel!*"

"Look, sorry, sorry, I'm still waking up. Just chill. I know *the rules* and this is *not* an emergency. We have *plenty* of food," he powered on past her disgusted grunt, "no technical failures, and we're headed for port. I'm sure everything will be back online long before we get there. You need to relax, enjoy the ride, and stop worrying!"

"You can't just ignore this!" She banged her fist on the table. "It won't just *magically* go away!"

Captain Bud sputtered for a moment, then stood and stormed off to the bridge.

"I swear," Ariel shouted at the now locked bridge door in frustration, "once we get back to the station, I'm going to make sure everyone knows what a *loser* you are!"

There was a ding from the kitchen as the printer completed her serving of tuna noodle casserole.

That evening, after pretending to fall asleep on the couch, Ariel waited patiently as Captain Bud snuck into the bedroom and locked the door triumphantly behind him. After a few extra minutes to make sure he wasn't coming back, she got up and headed to the bridge.

After spending so much time recently in the ramshackle living area, she was surprised at how plush the bridge actually was. Like the bedroom, it had antique-styled molding around a swirled plasterwork ceiling, and the walls were paneled with what appeared to be the same hardwood that covered the bedroom floor. The window at the front of the room was even surrounded by a swirling gilded frame with a roaring lion head at each corner, like something you might find around fine art in a museum.

The small bridge was also silent—everything was on mute, just the way Captain Bud liked it.

Ariel approached the main, and only, control station hoping to get independent confirmation of their situation, or at least a reliable ETA. She was surprised once again when the screen came on to display the full command interface, active and awaiting input. Across the top of the screen was the ETA she had been looking for:

Time to destination forty-four days

"No passcode, and so much for 'a couple of weeks,'" she scoffed. "Why am I even surprised? Communications."

A new window grew out of the **COMMUNICATIONS** indicator until it filled the screen. The communications window contained four indicators: **DATA FEEDS** in red; **SHIP-TO-SHIP**; **EMERGENCY BEACON**; and **EMERGENCY RECEIVER**, all in green.

"Emergency receiver status."

At her command, a new window started to expand out from the **EMERGENCY RECEIVER** indicator. It paused part-way through the process, reversed, then disappeared. The **EMERGENCY RECEIVER** indicator changed to red for a moment, a "Receiver not found" alert appearing, then quickly disappearing below it, then switching back to green.

"Emergency receiver status," she said again, her aggravation growing as the window repeated its disappearing act.

Pushing down her aggravation, she said, "Feed status."

The **DATA FEEDS** indicator expanded to fill the screen. The new window was titled "No Feeds Available," with two options below it:

Switch to alternate feed

Attempt to reconnect

"Alternate feed," she said, and was immediately disappointed by the response:

No alternate feeds configured

"Okay, reconnect." The screen responded to this with:

Connection failed - no signal detected

"Okay, we're already bending the rules, let's start *breaking* them. Back. Activate emergency beacon." The options shrank back into the **DATA FEEDS** indicator. The **EMERGENCY BEACON** indicator turned blue for a moment, then red, a "Beacon did not engage" message appearing, then immediately disappearing beneath it, then finally back to green.

"Ugh, okay. In for a penny, in for a pound," she said under her breath, then louder, "Activate SOS."

A new window grew out of the green **SHIP-TO-SHIP** indicator. The window was red and titled, "Applicable system status not found," with the message:

Please provide emergency documentation packet

"And where would I get one of those?" she asked herself.

She spent several minutes navigating through Captain Bud's poorly organized file storage but could find no hint of the necessary documentation or instructions to show how to create it.

"Okay, what now?" she asked herself in frustration.

After a moment in thought, she said, "Well, that Door setup looked pretty amateur. I should probably make sure it's actually plugged in, then figure out where the *captain* stores his Conduits."

Back in the living area, Ariel paused to sneer at the poorly installed Door before cautiously kneeling beside it and looking into the small gap behind the frame. She recoiled in disgust at the sight of a fuzzy object leaning against the power cable but quickly realized that it was just a moldy fruit peel.

"Don't look too close, just get the job done."

She flicked the peel away, then checked the power cable. It was secure, but her hand came away stained with an unidentifiable black substance. She stood, moved to wipe her hand off on her shirt, but thought better of it, and instead inspected the diagnostic cable. Despite being old and cracked, the cable did appear to be properly connected.

"Now, where's the most sensible place for the Conduits?" She laughed grimly. "And when you figure that out, put that location at the *end* of the list."

She opened the left door of the closest cabinet, the middle unit in a column of three. The right door, which didn't match, immediately canted sideways and swung open on one hinge loosely attached to its lower half. After a quick glance inside at a variety of shoes and boots, she carefully closed both doors together.

With far more caution, she opened the cabinet above it, which contained a variety of fashionable headwear hanging on pegs. She moved on.

Finally, in a drawer near the middle of the wall, just below Captain Bud surfing on a wave pool, she found what she was looking for: two Conduits, one red and one grey.

The Conduits were each plugged into makeshift mounts, which were attached to the ends of separate cables that snaked out through the drawer's missing rear panel. The light on the grey Conduit was red, and the one on the red Conduit was green.

Confused by the green status light, she picked up the emergency receiver first. It felt unusually light in her hand.

"Bad connection?" she wondered before unplugging it. The light went out immediately. "That's not right…" She plugged it back in, and the green light came back on just as fast. "…and neither is that."

Ariel unplugged the grey Conduit, having to use far more force than with the receiver due to the poor fit of the mount, and the status light faded out. After she worked it back into the mount and twisted it to the locked position, the status light started flashing yellow.

She started holding her breath but released it with a curse as the status light quickly turned red.

After dropping the Conduit into the drawer, she roughly shoved it closed in frustration. The drawer went in most of the way but then bounced out again—only a quick grab preventing it from falling out onto the floor.

It took her three more attempts to get the drawer closed as the loose Conduit cables repeatedly got caught between the drawer and the wall behind it, requiring her to reach in with one hand and carefully reposition them each time.

Once the drawer was finally shut, she returned to the bridge and tried the controls again but had no better luck than her first attempt.

"This whole ship is bocked!"

CHAPTER SEVEN

Eric Hamilton was carrying the two replacement distributors as the Hamilton family turned left into the short corridor between the bridge and the living areas. His wife Dianne was skimming over the instructions on her technician's screen while Violette bounded down half a level to the engineering landing.

"Let's start with the port distributor since it's right here," Violette suggested.

"Fine with me," her mother replied. "You know where power control is."

Violette slid open the door on the aft end of the landing, flipped on the lights, then headed down the narrow corridor.

The corridor ran through the port engineering control room and ended at a second door, which provided access to the port environmental systems room. Violette stopped at a wider section halfway between the two doors, where a rounded access cover was positioned on the right, cold-wall side below a large, wall-mounted screen. The access cover was labeled "Danger: Power Systems, do not open while engines are engaged."

When he arrived, Eric placed the blue boxes on the nearest of two shelves, which were mounted to the wall on either side of the cover.

"Okay," Dianne said, placing her screen on the farthest shelf and tapping on it. "Here are the instructions."

The screen on the wall above the access panel came on slowly to display a page titled, "Package Contents," with drawings of the pentagon-shaped distributer and a series of adapter disks. At the bottom of the screen was printed, "Adapter will vary depending on chosen installation package."

Dianne pulled out three wrenches and a multi-driver from the pocket on the front of her overalls and placed them on the shelf beside her tablet. "And here are the tools we'll need." She swiped twice on the wall screen. The first time displayed a page titled, "Tools Required," with drawings matching the three wrenches and driver. The second changed it to one titled, "Step One: Preparation."

"Engine off, check," she said, glancing at a large green status light on the wall just below the screen.

"Access cover open," Violette said, unlatching and removing the curved cover, then handing it off to her father, who stood it up against the wall farther up the corridor.

Under the cover was a small chamber with the five-sided distributer positioned right in the center. Three smaller rectangular devices sat on the right side, and three thick, black cables entered from the left. The three black cables were plugged into sides of the distributor labeled A, B, and C. Each of the rectangular units was connected to two blue cables on their shorter sides, with the largest of the rectangular units using thicker cables. One of each set of blue cables left the chamber, and the other connected to the distributer. The thicker of the blue cables, which was slightly thinner than the black ones, was plugged into the fourth side of the distributor, which was labeled 1. The two remaining blue cables were plugged into the final side, labeled 2.

"Check," her mother said. "Verify that distributor is offline."

Violette pointed to the green status light in the center of the distributor. "Check." She turned to the screen and said, "Next page!"

On the screen appeared a new page titled, "Step Two: Disconnect backup power."

"Okay, let's get started. Hand me the number 3 wrench."

Violette grabbed the largest of the wrenches, which had "n3" engraved on the handle, and handed it to her mother.

Dianne placed the wrench around the connector for the cable on the side labeled C. After a few turns with the wrench, she slid the locking nut off the threaded mount.

"Disconnect battery power," she said, as she pulled the cable loose. The light on the distributer changed to yellow.

"Check," Violette said. "Next page!"

The screen changed to, "Step Three: Disconnect main power."

"Okay, here's where I need some help," Dianne said, glancing at the page on the screen, which featured a large red warning:

Dual power sources must be disconnected simultaneously.

Failure to follow this instruction may cause permanent damage to the unit and is not covered by your warranty.

Authorized service technicians are recommended for any power system maintenance.

"I'll need each of you to hold one of the power cables in place while I remove the locking nuts. Once they're off, we disconnect them both at the same time. Got it?"

"Yep," Violette said, saluting.

"Sure thing, Captain," her father said, joining in.

"My loyal crew." Dianne rolled her eyes. "I hope this won't be too complicated for you."

"Nope." Violette grinned. "Yank as soon as it's loose."

"I am filled with confidence." Dianne started loosening the cable on the B side.

After a few turns, she slid back the securing nut, then repeated the procedure on the A side.

"Okay, now on three, pull out both power cables." She began counting. "One… Two… *Three!*"

Eric and Violette pulled on their cables, and the yellow light on the distributor blinked out.

"Good work," Dianne said. "Now we can disconnect the data lines."

"Next page," Violette told the screen.

The screen changed to display, "Step Four: Disconnect control interface."

"The number 4 wrench please," Dianne said, holding the first wrench out to her daughter.

Violette grabbed the next smallest wrench, engraved with "n4," and exchanged it for the larger one.

After Dianne removed the nut and disconnected the larger blue cable, Violette instructed the screen to change the page.

The new page read, "Step Five: Disconnect diagnostic interface."

"The number 6 wrench please," Dianne said, getting the smallest wrench, this one engraved with "n6," in exchange for the one she had just finished with.

"Next page," Violette said, after the first of the small blue cables was removed. "Step Six: Disconnect synchronization interface (multi-engine configurations only)" appeared on the screen.

Dianne removed the final cable and said, "Now we can remove the distributer."

After another "next page" command, the screen read, "Step Seven: Remove unit."

Following the instructions on the screen, Dianne twisted the five-sided distributor counterclockwise until it stopped then lifted it out, flipped it over, and sat it down on top of her technician's screen.

The next page was titled, "Step Eight: Connect adapter."

Eric opened the first of the two blue boxes and removed a plastic envelope that was sitting on top of the plastic wrapped distributer. He handed it to his wife, who removed a red disk from within it and handed that to her daughter. "Make sure it matches the one on the old distributer."

"Looks the same to me," Violette said, holding the new adapter beside the original. "They both say, 'JPD-506.'"

"In that case, I'll need the driver," Dianne said, over the noise of her husband pulling the new distributor from the box and unwrapping it.

Violette handed her the driver, and Eric handed her the unwrapped distributor. She lined up a notch in the adapter disk with a protrusion on the side of the indent on the bottom of the new distributor, then tightened the four pre-attached locking screws.

"Step Nine: Insert new unit."

After they twisted the new distributor into place and reversed the process to connect it, the status light went green, Eric replaced the lid, and Violette latched it shut.

As soon as the final latch was secure, the instructions faded from the screen and were replaced by a setup page. The first setup step appeared in the middle of the screen and was labeled, "Primary Power," with three options spaced out below it: A, B, and C.

"Now let's finish this," Dianne said, tapping on A. The options disappeared. "Primary Power" shrank, changed to "Primary Power: Port A," and moved to the upper left-hand corner of the screen.

A new step appeared in the center of the screen labeled "Primary Power Source," with a list of options: Fusion Class A, ZPG Class 1, ZPG Class 2, ZPG Class 3.

After Dianne tapped on "ZPG Class 2" it changed to "Primary Power Source: ZPG Class 2" and joined "Primary Power: Port A" in the upper left-hand corner of the screen.

The screen was now asking about "Secondary Power" with the same letter options but with A in grey. She tapped B, then "ZPG Class 2" on the follow-up screen.

"Backup Power" followed with the A and B options in grey and a new "none" option. Dianne tapped C.

The now familiar source screen appeared with a fifth option for "Battery," which she tapped.

Now "Control Interface" appeared with three options: 1, 2A, and 2B. She tapped 1.

"Diagnostic Interface" followed and 2A was tapped.

The options for the next "Engine Count" screen included single, paired, and quad. Dianne tapped paired.

When "Synchronization Data" appeared, Dianne tapped the only remaining option: 2B.

The final setting, "Engine Configuration," offered port aft, port forward, starboard aft, and starboard forward. She tapped port forward.

A **SAVE** button appeared on the screen.

"And save," Dianne said, as she tapped on it.

A few moments later, the screen went green and displayed a large "Configuration Saved" message.

"Okay, moment of truth," Dianne said, as the green screen was replaced with a yellow one labeled "Power System Ready" featuring a large **ACTIVATE** button.

After she tapped the button, five red icons appeared on the screen. A moment later, they all started flashing yellow. Almost immediately the first icon, a line drawing of the end of a cable, went green. The second, a drawing of the end of a cable with the letters "ABC" below it, also went green. After a few minutes, the third icon, a drawing of a checklist, went green. A few minutes later, the fourth icon, a drawing of a rocket ship, turned green immediately followed by the final icon, a drawing of an old-fashioned, two-handled control wheel.

"Perfect. Looks like I was worried about nothing. Let's move on to starboard."

The checklist icon for the starboard distributor turned red and error codes started scrolling down the display below it.

"Frag," Dianne muttered. "Trying again."

The icons went red again, then yellow, then the cable icon went green, followed by the ABC cable, then the red checklist and a waterfall of errors.

"Okay, let's go through the setup again."

They did, even stopping at the end to carefully match the list of selections in the upper left-hand corner of the screen to the configuration of the new distributer. The checklist icon stubbornly continued to turn red.

"Let's disconnect everything and make sure they're all seated correctly," Dianne said, with resignation.

They did and got another red checklist.

"Something's not right, and I can't see what." Dianne sighed. "It's getting late. Let's stop here, get some sleep, and try again tomorrow."

Over breakfast the next morning, Dianne announced, "I'm going to reset it to factory defaults and go through the setup again. I'm certain that it's installed properly and that we were doing the setup correctly so it must be the distributor—hopefully just a setting that didn't save completely. On the plus side, since the hard part is done, I'll be able to take care of it myself."

"I'll keep you company," her husband offered.

"I'll be in my room," Violette said, getting up and dropping her plates into the washer.

The message on the screen changed to "Reset complete. Starting firmware update."

"*Aha!* There was a stuck update! Enough of it must have installed to pass the diagnostics but not enough for it to actually work!" Her smile quickly faded.

"What?" Eric asked.

"I just realized," she said grimly, "if this update fails, we're in trouble. Normally I'd wipe it and do a clean install—but we can't exactly download a new installer right now."

"Can you copy the one that's already there?"

"No," she said, shaking her head. "Verified downloads are moved to a secure partition before they're allowed to load."

"What do we do if it fails?"

"We put the old one back in and push it until it dies. When it does, we hope that it doesn't fry the power system so that we can get a little more time with the old port distributor."

With a concerned look, Eric asked, "If it fries the power system, won't that take out both engines?"

"No." Dianne shook her head again. "It wouldn't get to the other engine. Even if it did, worst case, it would only kill the sync manager. I can deal with that. They always include an un-synced engine simulation on the recertification exams."

"And if the second distributor fails?" Eric asked, looking into his wife's eyes for reassurance.

"When," she corrected, before continuing more gently, "we'll have to drop the hold and limp in on just the port."

"Won't that take a lot longer?"

"Hopefully not a lot." She put her hand on his shoulder and squeezed. "It all depends on how much time we can get out of the starboard. We would broadcast an SOS that should draw in a patrol ship as we get closer to Ginhard. With luck, we'd be rendezvousing with the patrol ship at around the same time we would have been making port with the two new distributors."

There was a chirp from the wall as "Update Complete" was displayed briefly before being replaced by the setup screen.

"I have a good feeling about this," Eric said.

Dianne squeezed his shoulder again, then turned to the screen. She mumbled to herself as she tapped through the setup. "Primary port A, source ZPG, secondary port B, source ZPG, backup port C, battery, control port 1, diagnostics 2A, paired, sync 2B, starboard forward and save."

They both held hands as the progress bar crept towards completion.

When "Configuration Saved" appeared on the screen, Dianne turned to her husband and said, "Okay, fingers crossed," then tapped the **ACTIVATE** button.

"Toes, too," Eric replied, as the five icons appeared: red, flashing yellow, one green, two.

The wait for the third green icon was excruciating but eventually rewarded.

If the wait for the third icon was excruciating, the wait for the fourth was inhumane torture.

"That did it!" Dianne shouted, as the control wheel finally changed color. "Green across the board. Next stop, Ginhard!"

CHAPTER EIGHT

After awakening to another solitary day aboard the PCV *Faro*, Captain Alvin Faro headed to the kitchen with the intent to make a pleasant dream into a reality.

He started gathering the necessary cartridges: egg (both yolk and white), English muffin, ham and hollandaise—the last two of which were nearly empty.

Alvin never allowed himself to finish off the last component of any favorite food, unconsciously preferring the mental consolation of knowing that there was always one more serving. Normally this ended with the next grocery run, but now that there was no scheduled delivery date, he was finally breaking that habit.

With all the ingredients lined up on the counter, he opened the side of the printer and started populating the empty cartridge slots. After snapping the final cartridge into place within the printer, he shut the access door and stepped back.

"Jeeves!"

As bidden, his virtual robotic assistant appeared in the kitchen beside him, its arms folded behind its back and its blue eyes regarding Alvin calmly.

"Eggs Benedict this morning, please."

As the robot unfolded its arms, its screen appeared so that it could "input" the necessary information.

When it finished, it looked up at Alvin as the screen disappeared. "Program loaded. Your meal will be ready in two minutes."

The printer started clicking internally as the printheads shuffled around to assemble Alvin's breakfast.

"Thank you, Jeeves," Alvin said happily. "Dismissed."

The robot faded, and he waited anxiously for the long minutes to pass.

"I'm really looking forward to this, Maria," he said, as he paced the room. "It's been too long since I started the day off with a proper breakfast!"

He smiled again as the printer dinged completion, collected his plate and a fresh set of utensils, then moved into the dining room.

But just as he positioned his fork and knife so that they neatly bracketed the meal on either side, an unbidden memory washed over him, and his good mood was washed away by the flood.

He sat alone at the dining room table in his pajamas with his eyes squeezed tightly shut, but not tight enough to prevent the tears from streaming down his cheeks. His awareness was forced into the past....

It was the first night that he and Maria had lived together.

They had rented a well-located, two-floor single bedroom duplex. The bathroom and bedroom were on the second floor, both clipped on one side by the slanting roof. The ground floor contained a living room, full kitchen, and separate dining room. A laundry room, some lockable storage space, and lots of cobwebs were located in the shared basement.

They were in good spirits despite a long day of unpacking, and Alvin had gallantly allowed her to shower first while he swept out the first floor.

After he had returned from his turn in the shower, she handed him two sets of utensils for the table and started making dinner with their fancy new printer.

He quickly dropped the utensils on the table, then moved upstairs to reorganize his nightstand.

A short while later, Maria's upset voice rang out from the dining room. "Alvin, come in here, please."

He hurried down the stairway and rushed into the room. "What's wrong?!"

She gestured at the utensils on the table in front of her. They were sparkling and freshly printed, the knife pointing towards her, the fork pointing away, and the spoon sitting at an angle with its handle across the others.

"I'm not mad," she said, in a tone that indicated otherwise, "I just want to make something clear."

"Okay," Alvin hesitantly replied, with a mixture of relief and confusion.

Maria collected both sets of utensils, held them up, and looked directly into her new husband's eyes.

"Family dinners have always been very important to me," she said slowly and clearly, before walking back to her original position at the table. "My father always set the table with great care."

She looked down and carefully placed the fork point up on her left. "My mother always loved a properly set table."

The knife was then placed on the other side, point up and blade towards the fork, carefully positioned the exact same distance from the edge of the table and with just enough room for a full-sized plate in between. "The night after Mom passed, Dad was barely keeping it together, so I offered to make dinner."

She placed the spoon alongside the knife, carefully lining up the ends of the handles. "I had never really thought about it before then, but out of habit, I set the table exactly as he would have. Exactly the way Mom liked it."

Without looking up, she moved over to the second place at the table and started laying out the other set of utensils with just as much care.

"When my father came in for dinner, he saw the place settings and was finally able to cry for Mom." She paused as a bittersweet look crossed her face. "We were *both* finally able to cry for Mom."

Maria finished the second place setting and looked up at her husband, her eyes moist. "I cherish that memory. When we finally started to deal with our grief *together.*" She paused again and took a deep breath. "There is so much in life that we can never control. Controlling *this* helps keep me centered and reminds me of family."

Alvin moved close and put his arms around her. "I'm sorry, I didn't know."

"Of course not." Maria sniffed and forced a small laugh. "If you had, I'd have been screaming at you."

"And I'd have deserved it." He chuckled as he squeezed her. "I promise that I'll do it properly from now on."

"You'd better." Maria squeezed him in return, then stepped back and wiped her eyes. "But, while we're at it, promise me something else."

With his hands on her shoulders, Alvin looked into her eyes. "Anything."

"Promise that we'll be honest with each other. That we'll always talk through our feelings together." There was an almost desperate firmness in her as she continued. "That everything will be out in the open, and we'll never let anything linger long enough to become a problem."

"Always, my love," Alvin had replied sincerely. "We'll have no secrets."

Alvin kept both of his promises.

After years of marriage, discussing their feelings every day became a natural part of their relationship. Insidiously and unconsciously, that forum also became the only place where Alvin could freely talk about his feelings.

He had discovered this limitation shortly after Maria's death when he attempted to discuss his anguish with friends who had gone through similar losses. To his dismay, he found that he could never quite make himself open up and that his half of the conversation was limited to banalities, like how quiet the house was.

To compensate, he had continued his discussions with Maria, and at the start, it felt good—like a form of therapy. Now it felt like desperation.

"Oh, Maria," he cried, "I can't even decide whether I'm happy that you didn't have to go through this or upset that you left me to go through it alone."

Alvin looked down at his plate as if he hadn't seen it before. After a moment, and despite the fact that the hollandaise sauce had long since cooled into a thick skin, he picked up his knife and fork and started cutting politely into his meal.

He ate in silence for several minutes, managing to control himself well enough that only the occasional tear escaped.

Eventually, the escaping tears were joined by another sob.

"I almost wish I had the courage to disable the sensors on the shuttle deck and open the pressure curtain." He paused, as if listening. "I know, I know. That's the coward's way out, and you'd never forgive me."

He lifted another cold fork-full of egg, Canadian bacon, and English muffin to his mouth with his right hand and wiped away another tear with his left.

When he was finished chewing, he looked up at the ceiling and said, "Don't worry, love, I won't give up no matter how badly I'm tempted."

CHAPTER NINE

Ariel had barely slept after her covert visit to the PLV *Rockhard*'s bridge, and it wasn't solely due to the uncomfortable couch.

Whirling thoughts of her discoveries and scenarios of their dire consequences fed her anxiety and kept her mind spinning throughout the night.

What little sleep she managed was steeped in despair and isolation, repeatedly marred by dreams of falling that ended with her jumping or rolling off the couch.

It was near the end of one of these dreams that Captain Bud, as he usually did after winning the nightly bedroom battle, rose early to start his monopolization of the bathroom as he went through his daily grooming routine.

She heard the shower as the floor woke her and wondered, not for the first time, why he still bothered.

After an impatient wait, she accosted him the instant the bathroom door started to slide open.

"Your beacon won't respond, and your emergency receiver won't engage!"

Captain Bud stopped in the bathroom doorway with a look of shock on his face. The look was due both to the angry and unexpected voice and the fact that he had nearly lost his towel as he skidded to a halt.

"How do you..." Captain Bud's protest was interrupted by the bathroom door striking him in the left buttock. He hopped forward as he continued. "Alice, were you messing around on *my* bridge?"

"*Ariel!*" Her face was getting red. "And I decided to stop waiting for you to start acting like the captain you *tell* everyone you are and take care of emergency protocols *myself!*"

"It's *illegal* for anyone but *the Captain* to do that!" Captain Bud blustered. "You had no right to access *my* system!"

"Then you shouldn't have disabled *your* security." She gave him an angry stare. When he finally wilted under it, she continued in an admittedly forced but reasonable tone. "Now, why won't the receiver engage?"

Captain Bud shifted uncomfortably and prayed for a reprieve, but all he received was another angry glare.

"Well," he responded sheepishly, "that's because it's just a shell with a light on the end."

Her eyes widened involuntarily, and her face grew more flush.

Seeing her reaction, Captain Bud's eyes widened just as involuntarily before he hastened to add, "I could never justify the cost of a real one."

She growled in frustration, but he pushed on.

"They're expensive!"

Ariel's angry sputtering demonstrated that she wasn't being placated.

Uncomfortable with his inability to gain control of the conversation, Captain Bud took a step back to give himself more space to think.

His movement proved counterproductive, as it helped Ariel to focus her anger. "And the door beacon?" she asked menacingly, as she followed his retreat.

"I looped the beacon…" He held his hands out in a defensive gesture.

"What?!" Ariel advanced on him again.

"C'mon, I'm never more than a few weeks out from the station." He stepped back, desperately searching for the right words.

The words he found were, "The Door was an *amazing deal!*"

"Not if it doesn't *work!*" Ariel growled in his face.

"It *works* fine!" he responded, stepping back yet again. "My friend got it for me *way* below cost! The *only* thing wrong with it was the beacon…"

Another growl.

"Look." Captain Bud tried to strike a reassuring tone. "The inspectors don't care if the beacon actually *works,* just that the diagnostics report—"

"I care!" she interrupted, advancing another step towards him. "And that's *not* the point! The *point* is that we're stuck out here, and we can't even let anyone know!"

Backing off, Captain Bud continued in his quickly faltering, reassuring tone. "We'll be at the station in no time!"

"'No time' being *weeks*. We need help *right now!*" Ariel's face fell and filled with despair.

Captain Bud, sensing an opening and regaining some confidence, said, "C'mon, we don't really need help." He forced a confident smile onto his face. "We'll get there. Just relax and enjoy the ride."

Ariel's face switched back to anger, and she was about to explode again but stopped suddenly as an idea occurred to her. "You've been insisting on making all of the meals."

"Just trying to be a good host!" he responded happily, taking her change of topic as a successful de-escalation.

"They've all been meal kits," she continued, working her way through the thoughts that were roiling in her mind. "I haven't seen you print anything that would have come from standard emergency supplies." She paused with a frown. "In fact, I've never seen anything other than meal kits…"

"The crawl space really is nasty," Captain Bud replied defensively, taking another step back. He frantically searched again for the right thing to say, finally coming up with, "The emergency supplies are as good as ever!"

"How good?" She stepped towards him. He attempted to retreat again but failed, discovering with a thump that he had backed himself into the wall of the bedroom on the far side of the corridor.

"Okay, empty boxes…" He stepped sideways to escape and quickly added, "But as long as the inspector sees something that looks…"

"Auuuug!" She raised her fists in frustration and lurched towards him with fury in her eyes.

Captain Bud quickly raised his hands again to protect his face. "Look, there are plenty of meal kits. *I swear* we won't run out!"

"More *chili fries?!*"

He started to search for the right calming words, drew a blank, then another, finally gave up, cleared his throat, then tried honesty. "Another fifteen cases…"

"*Auuuug!*"

"But not *just* chili fries…" He withered again under her glare but struggled on to his point. "There are more burgers… and noodles…" He stopped, realizing with dismay that he had run out of information.

"This was all *such* a bad idea!" Ariel started grabbing at her hair as she stomped back into the living area. "I can't *believe* that I fell for that captain line. I should *never* have stepped foot on this ship!" She turned back to Captain Bud and pointed an accusing finger at him. "I should have turned around the *moment* I saw that crappy little *cold-wall* Location of yours!"

CHAPTER TEN

"Ugh," Violette Hamilton exclaimed, as she slumped onto the couch. "If I have to stay cooped up in here any longer, I'm going to *just die!*"

Across the room, Eric Hamilton stiffened and, before he realized it was happening, shouted back, "Stop complaining! We're all cooped up here, *not just you!*"

"I was just joking," Violette said, with a hurt expression.

"This is *not a joke!*"

"I know, but…" Violette's eyes welled with tears.

Realizing that he was being unfair but finding himself completely unable to strike a more reasonable tone, Eric fled from the room.

"We'll talk about this later!" he shouted over his shoulder as he rushed into the corridor.

Violette looked after her father in shock, the tears now pouring down her cheeks.

Eric entered the bedroom and roughly tapped a six-digit code into the Pad beside the door. The twelve number keys sank back into the Pad and were replaced by a red padlock shape.

"Did you just lock…" Dianne started, pausing in surprise as her husband leaned back against the door and slid down to the floor.

"Are you all right?" she shouted, jumping off the bed and rushing to his side. "Did something happen? Is Violette okay?"

"I'm sorry, I'm sorry," he sobbed. "I thought I was okay… I barely made it here before…"

"Did something happen?" she asked again, more forcefully this time.

"No… yes… not really…" He struggled to collect his thoughts. "I think I'm losing it…"

"Is Violette okay?" she asked in a gentler tone, as she lifted his head to look into his eyes.

"Yes, yes…" he said, pushing away her hands, dropping his head and starting to shake. "It's me… I'm…"

"It's okay," she responded, taking his dark hands in her pale ones. "We all deal in our own way. Take a moment to breathe."

He nodded and took a deep shuddering breath.

"That's it," she said, settling down beside him. "In and out. Take as long as you need."

To cover the sounds of her husband's deliberate but shuddering breathing, Dianne started her own confession. "I knew it was something big right away but kept trying to convince myself that I was wrong."

"I think we all did," Eric said softly, having regained a little of his composure.

"I know I've been short a lot lately, especially with Violette."

"The two of you are always short with each other."

Dianne enfolded him in her arms.

"We need to stop pretending that things are still normal," Eric said with conviction.

"I agree. What are you thinking?"

"That we need to take a moment to talk about how we're feeling."

"I think that's a great idea." Dianne squeezed him. "We can talk all night if you want."

Eric shook his head. "No, it needs to be as *a family,* not just the two of us."

"I don't want to upset Violette," Dianne said softly. "I hate that she has to go through this."

"But she *is* going through this." He paused in thought. "Perhaps we can all talk over dinner?"

Dianne nodded in agreement. "You're right, of course. I'm still not out of the habit of thinking of her as our little girl."

"She's fifteen now and, I'm certain, in just as much pain as we are."

"It's nearly dinner time now." Dianne squeezed him again. "I'll go get Violette, and you can take a little time to collect yourself."

"No, let me talk with Violette," he said, extracting himself from her arms. He kissed her on the forehead and started to rise. "I need to let her know that we're still okay. That we're all still on the same side." He reached down to help his wife up. "She's probably in the shuttle."

"Violette?" Eric called through the open hatch of the shuttle.

"I'm not here," Violette's voice replied quietly.

"Please, can we talk? I'm sorry about before. This is all getting to me and—"

"It's getting to me, too!" Violette appeared in the open hatchway, her eyes red and puffy and her cheeks damp. She was shaking and holding her arms stiffly at her sides as she shouted, *"I can't do this alone!"*

Tears flowed from them both as Eric stepped forward to embrace his daughter tightly.

"You won't have to," he said, stroking her hair. "I can't do this alone either."

She looked up at him with a hesitant smile on her face as he continued. "Your mother and I have decided that it's time to bring everything out in the open. When you're ready, come up for dinner, and we'll *all* take turns talking."

"I think I'd like that." Violette stepped back and wiped her face.

Eric wiped his face and laughed. Violette looked up at him quizzically.

"You didn't find any more beef stroganoff while you were in there, did you?"

Violette started to giggle uncontrollably at his comically hopeful expression.

"You know it's my favorite!" he added, grabbing her shoulders and craning his neck to glance past her into the shuttle.

Violette laughed out loud, then buried her face in her father's chest.

As the last of the dinner was consumed, the dining room fell into an awkward silence that lasted until Eric finally spoke up. "Okay, I said I wanted us to talk, so it's only fair that I go first."

After a pause to collect himself, he continued. "Ever since we found out that the station was gone, I've been feeling like the walls are closing in and that I'm alone in the universe."

Violette and Dianne spoke as one. "You are *not* alone!"

He smiled weakly at his family, greatly reassured by their joint support. "I know it's not rational, but it's how I feel, and it's time to put all of our fears, real or not, on the table." He looked down at the table between them. "So to speak."

He paused again as a look of pain crossed his face. "I've been having nightmares every night. In some you're both gone or dead or both, and in others I find myself trapped in a tiny room. When I escape, I end up in an even smaller room, but I keep trying until I end up in a coffin, my cries for help drowned out by the sound of dirt piling on top of me."

His family looked horrified.

Dianne reached across the table and took his hand. "We're here."

Violette reached over and, with great discomfort, patted her father briefly on the arm before saying, "I understand now."

He squeezed her shoulder. "I'm still sorry about that."

"I know."

The room fell quiet again as Eric tried to banish the haunted look from his face.

Dianne broke the silence. "As I told your father earlier, deep down I knew this was big right from the start, but I was so afraid that you'd both fall apart if I broke out of my unshakable captain role that I couldn't even admit it to myself."

Violette looked confused. "When have you been *unshakable?*" At her father's look, she quietly said, "Sorry."

"I had a dream last night that there was something vital that I had to do," Dianne continued, as if her daughter had never spoken. "I picked up my screen and tapped on the control but realized that it was just a sticker. I peeled it off only to discover another sticker beneath it. Once I got that sticker off, I tapped the control again, but nothing happened. I kept frantically tapping it until the control window finally opened. But, instead of finally being able to get anything done, I discovered that it was yet another sticker. I feel like a fraud."

"You're *so* not a fraud!" Violette interjected. "You do so much with work and the ship. I wish I could be *half* the person you are!" She suddenly looked embarrassed.

Dianne laughed and patted her daughter on the arm. "Relax, I didn't hear a thing."

"Then I'll repeat it," Eric said, then continued slowly, clearly enunciating each word. "You are *not* a fraud."

Dianne smiled. "Maybe not, but I've never been more than a casual captain. I could always call on someone who actually knew what they were doing if anything went wrong. Now, it's just me."

"We would never be where we are right now without you," Eric said reassuringly. "You're a great captain. I don't even want to think what it would be like if we didn't have someone like you keeping everything running."

"Thanks, but look at the emergency supplies," Dianne said, gesturing towards the dirty dishes, then flicking a crumb of protein bar off the table. "If I'd kept on top of those, we might have just finished a *real* dinner."

"That wasn't you," Eric replied seriously. "I'm the one who does the shopping. How many times did you ask me if the supplies were okay, and how many times did I tell you they were fine?"

"I suppose that's true," she replied grudgingly. "I still should have checked them myself."

"Me, too."

"I don't blame either of you," Violette said seriously, then smiled. "I blame *the printer!*"

Dianne rolled her eyes and smiled back weakly.

"Well, Violette," her father prompted, "since you piped up, why don't you tell us how you're feeling?"

Violette looked uncomfortable, made several false starts, then finally blurted, "It's all just so *unfair!*"

As she started crying, her parents, seated on either side of her, both leaned over to put a hand on her shoulder.

She brushed them off. "I'm okay, I'm okay." She straightened, but her face was as full of despair as her eyes were full of tears. She continued with a quavering voice, "I had so much that I wanted to do! Now I'm so afraid that I'll never get to do anything but die here."

Her parents looked at each other with pained expressions, and both had to stop themselves from placing their hands reassuringly back onto her shoulders.

"I keep thinking that something else is going to happen," Violette said. "Something *worse!* That we'll *never* get to Ginhard. That I'll *never* see my friends again. That I'll *never* get a chance to grow up!"

"Oh, Violette, I'm so sorry," her mother said, with a ragged voice. "Clearly we're all feeling trapped."

She reached out to her daughter, who finally consented to a hug.

When the hug was finally broken off, Eric said, "We can't lose hope. When we feel trapped, we have to remember that we're trapped *together.* And as long as we're *together,* I know that we'll get through this."

CHAPTER ELEVEN

Captain Alvin Faro instinctively leapt out of bed at the buzz of the PCV *Faro*'s emergency alarm.

Naval training and a lifetime of muscle memory carried him quickly and unerringly to the bridge. He was barely awake when he dropped into his command chair, unconsciously double tapping his wristband to activate the controls.

Instead of the expected virtual controls, the only response to his taps was another floating "Critical System Failure" notice, this time reading:

Primary Zero-Point Generator offline

Secondary Zero-Point Generator output dropping - filament failure in process

Battery power below 5%

Emergency power protocol in effect

Safe navigation protocol in effect

Engines disengaging

Communications failure - no response from emergency support

Emergency beacon activation failed

Immediate alternate power source required

Ship status updated

SOS broadcast activated

"Being stubborn isn't going to change anything," Alvin said to the warning, as he angrily swiped his hand through it.

He flicked at the notice repeatedly, but it refused to budge. While he was flicking, a panel in the floor in front of his chair slid back, and a tactile control panel rose through the opening to position itself above Alvin's lap. The control panel was a smaller and more cramped version of his usual virtual ones.

"Jeeves!"

After a moment, he looked around in surprise before comprehension dawned. "Of course, power protocol, no more Jeeves."

He glanced at the physical control panel in front of him for the first time.

"I am *not* my father," Alvin said, as he tapped a green indicator labeled **AUDIO INTERFACE,** which was positioned between the red **HOLOGRAPHIC INTERFACE** indicator and the blue **TACTILE INTERFACE** indicator. "I'll talk to the air. It's what all the kids are doing nowadays anyhow."

"Audio interface activated," a plain, artificial voice answered, as the control panel's tactile control surfaces folded underneath its screen.

"Override critical system failure notice."

At Alvin's command, the warning disappeared.

"How much of our itinerary is remaining?"

"Eight days," the voice reported, as the current itinerary appeared on the screen.

Like the tactile controls, this version of the itinerary was similar to the presentation that Alvin was accustomed to, but limited to the progress line and distance details. A blue dot sat between the green completed sections of the flight path and the four red incomplete sections between the *Faro* and Ginhard.

"Are we in range of the system buoys?"

"Negative." The final two line segments flashed to indicate the extent of the buoys' range.

"Can we pull power from the cargo container?"

"Negative. There are no power connections between this vessel and the container."

"Can we transfer the ZPG from the container?"

"Negative. The Zero-Point Generator would not fit into the cargo elevator."

"Can we transfer the ZPG externally?"

"Negative. The Zero-Point Generator is too large for you to move by hand. It would not fit into the shuttle, and the shuttle has no external cargo clamps."

"Status of shuttle."

"PCV *Faro* shuttle 1 is fully charged and ready for pre-flight checks." The voice paused briefly, then continued. "However, the shuttle does not have sufficient range to reach the Ginhard system."

"How close can we get?" Alvin leaned his head back against the command chair's headrest and closed his eyes.

The first red line segment turned blue, and the second, yellow, as the voice responded, "The shuttle will be able to cover one-third of the remaining distance."

"Will that get us in range of the buoys?"

"Negative." The final two line segments flashed again unseen.

"I'll just have to hope for a patrol." Alvin opened his eyes and began to stand. As he did so, the control panel bent forward at the base to give him more room. "Begin pre-flight checks on the shuttle and download a flight plan to Ginhard."

Three hours later, Alvin painfully dumped a final cart-full of emergency supplies into the central area of the shuttle—they landed in a pile against the weight of a stack of newly-printed water bottles. He blindly pushed the cart back into the shuttle bay, where it rolled freely until it struck the bulkhead on the opposite side of the room with a muted thud.

He started to pick up one of the boxes, moaned, dropped it, then said to himself, "No rush, I'll have plenty of time to clean up later."

He shuffled over to the table, then sat for a while rubbing his sore arms and breathing heavily.

Once he caught his breath, he returned to the *Faro*'s bridge via the elevator to complete the final steps of his evacuation.

"Enter an abandoned ship status in the log and update the SOS packet. Once the shuttle is clear, power down all systems except the ship-to-ship transmitter. That should keep it going for a few days," Alvin ordered, then started to rise.

"Acknowledged," the system's voice responded, as the control screen folded forward.

"Well, Maria," Alvin said sadly, as he took in the dull grey room, "she was good to us. I hope whoever claims the salvage won't just scrap her."

After wiping his eyes, Captain Alvin Faro then left the bridge of the PCV *Faro* for the final time.

When he arrived back at the shuttle, he headed directly to the small bridge. As he settled into the narrow control chair, he realized that the shuttle, which he had picked up from a naval surplus yard but never actually flown, had only the military-standard tactile controls.

"You win, Dad," he said, as he flipped the physical **POWER** switch.

The control panel lit up, along with a status screen in front of him, which immediately displayed a report:

Itinerary downloaded

Flight plan accepted

Pre-flight checks passed

PCV *Faro* shuttle 1 ready for departure

Alvin stretched his arm to reach the dock interface board, located all the way over on the far-right side of the control panel and separated by a raised red border, and toggled the **DOCK PRESSURIZATION** switch off.

The screen in front of him went red, and the status report was replaced with:

Warning: dock depressurizing

Outer door controls now disabled

After a few minutes of silence, a shudder passed through the shuttle as the shuttle bay's pressure curtain released its grip and slid aside.

He reached out again, stopping just short of the dock interface board, where he toggled the **GROUND HOVER** switch to on.

There was a much smaller shudder as the shuttle lifted a short distance off the bay's deck.

Alvin pushed the **ENGINE POWER** slider up a tiny fraction of its range, and the shuttle moved slowly out into space.

On the screen, a diagram appeared displaying outlines of the shuttle and the front edge of the *Faro*. When the oval representing the shuttle cleared the curved outline of the *Faro*'s nose less than a minute later, it disappeared and was replaced with a view of the *Faro* as seen from the rear of the shuttle.

Alvin toggled **GROUND HOVER** back to off then watched the *Faro* grow dark as his virtual assistant executed his final orders.

With great regret, he started to move the shuttle back into the shipping lane and out to a safe distance where he could engage the hyperdrive. The *Faro* started to quickly shrink once he pushed the **ENGINE POWER** slider up to full.

The PCV *Faro* was barely visible against the dark backdrop of space when Alvin toggled the **HYPERDRIVE** switch and it shrank away to nothing.

CHAPTER TWELVE

It had been nearly a week since they had been disconnected from the station, and the atmosphere aboard the PCV *Rockhard* had gotten downright depressing.

Without a feed, Captain Bud was limited to his collection of data chips filled with downloaded content, and they were getting repetitive. Most of these chips contained shows that he'd borrowed from friends who subscribed to channels that he wasn't willing to pay for. The rest of the chips, the ones he was most proud of, were illicit recordings of live, no-streaming concerts.

With his distractions failing, he was beginning to experience difficulties dealing with increasingly strong urges that couldn't be fully satisfied during alone time.

He knew he had to take direct action.

It had been a difficult process, but Captain Bud finally worked out a plan to get things back on track.

For step one, he moved over to the printer and slapped the Pad on its side to activate it.

"Display my 'Impressem' collection," he said with grandeur.

A holographic projector built into the top of the printer generated half a dozen quarter-scale images of Captain Bud, each wearing a different outfit. The body of each image turned slowly back and forth to show off the clothes while the heads remained locked in place, staring straight ahead.

"Too last season," he said, flicking away the figure all the way on the left. Another Captain Bud in a different outfit appeared to replace it. "No, too blue." He flicked that one away as well.

He continued flicking away options until there were just three remaining. As his eyes fell on the central outfit, his face brightened.

"Perfect!" he said, admiring the smaller version of himself and using both hands to flick away the other two. "That one has never failed me! Scan and print!"

The sizing rod moved out to the front of the printer, and a thin section along the front of it lit up in bright blue. Captain Bud followed the repeated "turn ninety degrees" instructions until the sizing rod went dark and moved back to its original position. He waited eagerly as the countdown clock ticked off the seconds while his selected outfit was put together.

He donned the clothes before they even had a chance to cool, then spent a long session in front of a holographic mirror, picking lint off this and straightening out that until he was finally satisfied.

After a final check of his breath in his cupped right hand, he strutted through the bedroom door.

His plan almost ended abruptly when he saw that Ariel was sitting on the couch reading one of his collectable 20th century magazine reproductions. The magazine was worth a fortune, having been printed (as in the ancient usage of the term) with pigmented inks on actual wood pulp paper. It wasn't meant to be taken from its protective case much less actually *read*.

Captain Bud had to fight down his reaction once again as he noticed a small tear in the back cover. Before today, that magazine had been worth more than three times what he had paid for it, but now he wouldn't even be able to sell it for half of what it cost!

Swallowing his umbrage for the greater good, Captain Bud forced the image of the damaged magazine out of his mind and a smile onto his face.

He sat down on the opposite end of the couch from his companion, smiled past her scowl, and focused on the plan.

"Look," he said in an apologetic tone, "I know things have been hard and there has been some tension…"

"Tension?!" Ariel said, rolling her eyes with disbelief. "You trap me here, feed me nothing but cheap meal kits, then refuse to send for help. Tension doesn't cover it!"

"Perhaps you're right," Captain Bud said humbly.

She looked back at him in surprise.

"No, no," he continued reassuringly. "I agree with you that the tension was partly my fault..."

"Partly?!"

"Okay, mainly," he agreed grudgingly, for the greater good, "but we need to get along or this trip is going to drive us both crazy."

"Assuming it hasn't already."

Captain Bud laughed good naturedly. "I don't think it has. You're just having a quite understandable reaction to our situation and," he added with calculation, "my poor behavior."

"So, you'll send the SOS now?"

"Of course," Captain Bud agreed quickly, "as soon as we finish working through this."

"What is there to work through?"

"I just think that we need to lower the tension level here so that we can both get through this. I want to do whatever's necessary to get back to a more friendly relationship."

"If you're going to be more reasonable that *might* be possible. Sending the SOS could certainly be a first step."

"As I said, it will be broadcasting as soon as we're done here."

"The sooner the better."

Captain Bud cleared his throat and continued. "I really think that, under the circumstances, we should try a clean start, make the best of what we have."

"Okay," she replied warily.

"We're both clearly stressed, and there's not really enough room here to get away from each other."

"That's for sure!" Ariel replied, unconsciously attempting to move past the arm of the couch, which was pressed against the small of her back.

"You and I had an amazing time that first night."

She gave him an incredulous look. "Amazing might be stretching it."

Captain Bud pushed on past the insult. "I truly believe that if we can just put aside our differences long enough for some intimate time it would do wonders for the both of us."

"Sorry, no." Ariel laughed uncomfortably. "Even if I was utterly desperate, I wouldn't be interested in any more *intimate time* with you."

"C'mon, we both need to relax a bit." He paused and put on his best smile. "We could have a good thing here." Captain Bud gently stroked her knee. "Don't play hard to get—"

Ariel's reaction was anything but gentle. She grabbed his wrist, stood, and violently twisted his arm. "Keep your hands to yourself, *Captain!*"

"I'm sorry! I'm sorry!" Captain Bud struggled to figure out what he had done wrong. "Just let go!"

Ariel released his arm and shoved him away in a single motion.

"I do think we need to get along," he said, as he regained his balance.

"We'll get along if you send out the SOS!"

"Yeah, yeah, I'll take care of it," he replied sulkily, and retreated to the bridge.

INTERLUDE

The Space Defense Alliance patrol ship *Audace* returned to normal space as its hyperspeed spatial distortion field collapsed at the edge of the Prosperity Corporate Zone. The ship sent an automatic status query to the nearest border buoy as it throttled down its main engines and came to a stop.

The VPS *Audace* was a large and boxy ship, with four engine pods, one attached to each corner of the rectangular aft two-thirds of its hull. The narrower front end of the ship sloped down from just behind the front tips of the top engine pods and ended with the main bridge, which protruded slightly farther than the large, segmented flight deck doors below it. The doors sloped slightly backwards towards the bottom of the ship and provided access to both flight decks (normally allocated with shuttles on the smaller lower deck and fighters above), as well as the eight hangar decks behind them. On either side of the ship's nose, just below the windows of the bridge, was the stylized image of a gondola that represented the planet Venice, its home port.

Patrol class spacecraft made up the majority of the fleet of naval ships and municipal boats that patrolled the vastness of interstellar space. While municipalities were concerned only with their own systems and the local ends of established shipping lanes, Naval ships like the *Audace* were found throughout the human sectors.

Scout class spacecraft, with their cylindrical design and lack of Zero-Point Generators (features that allowed them to pass through Portals instead of crawling between systems at hyperspeed), made up the rest of the fleet—with one exception.

That exception was the sole assault class ship still in operation, the ΔAS *General Patton*, which hadn't left the Terra Delta system since it had become the operational headquarters of the SDA Navy.

The Space Defense Alliance had been founded shortly after the Second Wave of Human Expansion with two goals. The first was to extend the original First Wave Coalition so that it included the newly established Second Wave sectors. The second, and the one that inspired the name, was to respond to growing security concerns, including the potential danger posed by intelligent alien life, an increase in piracy along newly extended and lonely shipping lanes, as well as high tensions that looked to be heading to war between several neighboring planets and sectors. These fears were used to justify the establishment of the assault class of ships in the SDA shipping codes, ships intended to transport large forces that could handle threats both in space and planet-side.

While the latter two security concerns were based on solid evidence, the idea that humanity was in danger of imminent alien invasion had been based on increasingly frequent sightings of huge and aggressive looking alien craft in the coreward most Wave Two sectors. After First-Contact, however, humanity learned that the Pterom were unarmed and had no ill-intent.

The main volume of the Pterom's large spacecraft was an open central area that allowed the flying species access to the single surrounding deck containing all their work and living areas. The aggressive appearance was pure anthropomorphism, misinterpreting the ruggedness of design necessary to contain their high-pressure ammonia atmosphere and the externalized nature of their ship systems.

Rather than being hostile, the Pterom were mainly indifferent towards mankind, as humanity was to them after getting over its initial panic. Neither species competed for living space and, being truly alien to each other, shared few mutual interests. A non-interference agreement was quickly established.

With the exception of two systems containing cultural exchange stations for their respective academics, they rarely interacted and never cohabitated within systems. Because of this, no territorial border was ever established, and both species overlapped their range in all of, in human terms, the coreward Wave Three sectors and several of the coreward Wave Two sectors.

Since that time, humanity encountered two other equally incompatible races with similar results.

Eventually, aside from the *General Patton*, the assault class ships were scrapped, many having never been deployed, and their parts recycled towards additional patrol ships.

"The network is down," Lieutenant Jamie Cooke, the VPS *Audace*'s detection officer on duty said, as the border buoy responded to their query. "No live status. Pulling the logs now."

Lieutenant Diogo de Abreu, communications officer on duty, reported next. "I'm detecting multiple SOSs and several emergency beacon mayday transmissions from the station."

"Make sure that Cartography logs those beacons, starting with the weakest. They didn't wait for confirmation that there was anyone to actually hear them, so most likely they didn't wait at all—batteries will be running out sooner rather than later."

"Sir," Lieutenant Cooke interjected, "according to the logs there are indications of multiple nuclear explosions both within the station and at the Portal starting a few second before contact was lost."

"Anything in the logs about the *Stalwart* or *Stabiae*?" Captain Brugnaro asked.

"Just a recurring note in the hourly report indicating that πPS *Stalwart* and HSS *Stabiae* were at dock."

"Helm, set course for the nearest SOS," Captain Brugnaro ordered. "Communications, start triaging the rest and provide a prioritized list to Navigation for plotting. Detection, I want everything you can extract about this zone. Intrusion, cobble something together from what's left of the system network and get me a wider view."

Taking advantage of Captain Brugnaro's brief pause, Lieutenant de Abreu said, "We're not receiving responses from any of the broadcasting craft."

"You're authorized to query for system logs. Detection, deploy sensor drones to the station and Portal. If we're dealing with radiation, I want to know before we send crew in there. Navigation, I want flight plans for every active distress transmission. We will uphold our obligation to investigate craft in distress." Captain Brugnaro toggled a switch on the control panel in front of him. "Flight Control, prepare recovery squadrons with fighter escort, coordinate with Navigation."

A few minutes later, the *Audace* slowed from another hyperspeed trip at the source of the closest call for help.

"Let me see it," Captain Brugnaro ordered.

A virtual screen appeared in front of him showing a small white craft with a blue stripe down the back. All of the navigation lamps and the windows to the bridge were dark. The same image appeared simultaneously on a much smaller screen built into the military-standard tactile control surface in front of him.

"Detection, can you confirm the registry?"

"Yes, sir, hull markings indicate that it is the PTB *Staten Island*."

"Communications?" Captain Brugnaro asked, glancing towards the communications station located at the front of the bridge just starboard of the main window, which was still shuttered after their recent hyperspeed transit.

"Still no live acknowledgment, sir. Logs show that the boat went into emergency shutdown three weeks after the incident."

"Detection, current ship status?"

"The boat appears to be cold and drifting, sir."

"Flight control, send over an inspection pod for confirmation."

It took almost as long for *Audace* pod 5 to travel and dock with the PTB *Staten Island* than it had for the patrol ship to jump in from the edge of the system.

"No survivors," Chief Harold Brashear reported back a short while later from the bridge of the stricken boat. "It's barely above absolute in here. Life support is offline and has been for a while. A short-range transport like this wouldn't have had more than a few days of emergency supplies on board. The pilot must have panicked and tried to make a run for it. The boat dropped out of hyperspeed here when they ran out of fuel."

"Discontinue the SOS, set a recovery beacon, and return to the ship."

"Sir," Lieutenant de Abreu said, "one of the recovery flights has rendezvoused with another broadcasting craft. They report the vessel as cold and drifting."

"Our probe has arrived at the Portal," Lieutenant Cooke reported from the detection station to the port of command. "Readings confirm that it has been destroyed and that the debris field is hot. Radiation levels and debris trajectories are consistent with multiple fission explosions."

"Warn all flights to avoid the vicinity of the station and Portal and to continuously scan for irradiated debris," Captain Brugnaro said. "Let's make sure not to add to the losses. How long until the probe arrives at the station?"

"Another hour, sir," Cooke answered.

"Redirect the probe along the main shipping corridor back to the station."

"Probe is on course to the station."

A few minutes later, Lieutenant Cooke looked up from her station. "The probe is detecting a cluster of craft near the midpoint of the shipping corridor." She paused as more information scrolled by on her screen. "Several craft are docked to a maintenance tug, two more are clamped to the hauling arms, and several more are positioned nearby."

"Is it broadcasting?"

"Not that the probe can detect, sir. The craft appears cold but stationary."

"Have the probe continue on to the station." Captain Brugnaro turned to Commander Junetta Morris, the ship's executive officer. "Dispatch a recovery flight to investigate."

"The recovery crew has detached the first craft from the tug." Lieutenant de Abreu relayed the reports coming from Flight Control. "Tug 2 is moving it out to a safe distance. "Shuttle 9 has docked with the tug and is transferring power now. Main computer is online, and the logs are downloading. The tug is identified as Prosperity Station tug 14. Recovery crew one is moving in. According to the tug's logs, power was exhausted less than a week ago."

After a surprised pause, Captain Brugnaro asked, "How could they have lasted that long?"

"According to the logs, when the last craft started running out of fuel, the maintenance engineers collected every emergency receiver and used the class 5 ZPGs from those to keep the environmentals running.

They also reconfigured a concessions printer on one of the transport boats to use matter from the main recycling system."

Captain Brugnaro closed his eyes for a moment. "XO, make sure to note their dedication and resourcefulness in the log. We may have been too late to help, but they still deserve recognition."

"Yes, sir," Commander Morris replied grimly.

"The final manual log entry contains several hundred personal messages," Lieutenant de Abreu reported.

"Forward them to command immediately."

"Getting a response from the station probe now," Lieutenant Cooke reported. "Readings are consistent with what we saw at the Portal but indicate a much larger number of explosions. I don't see a single intact module and very few large pieces of debris. The probe is logging multiple mayday beacon transmissions that were too weak to detect from the edge of the zone. It's also receiving a tracking signal from the HSS *Stabiae*'s flight recorder."

"Will we be able to recover it?" Brugnaro asked.

"Recover, no," Lieutenant Cooke answered without looking up. "But I can task the probe to collect the data. It should survive the radiation long enough for a download, and the second probe can continue scanning the area when it arrives."

The probe captured the HSS *Stabiae*'s flight recorder an hour later and immediately started to broadcast the encrypted recording back to the ship.

"Sir, the flight recorder data has been decrypted," Lieutenant Cooke reported. "The sensors recorded explosions and radiation just before the *Stabiae* disintegrated. Defensive systems automatically logged some debris trajectories that appear to indicate that the explosions originated on the Collection level."

Captain Brugnaro rose and signaled to Commander Morris. "I'll be in my cabin for a bit. While I'm gone, put together an emergency message. I'll deliver it from my office as soon as it's ready."

CHAPTER THIRTEEN

Every screen aboard the PCV *Hamilton* flashed red, then displayed the ten-pointed star logo of the Space Defense Alliance.

"It's an emergency transmission!" Violette Hamilton shouted, jumping off the couch so fast that she had to take three steps before she caught her balance. *"Finally!"*

"I'll put it on the entertainment screen." Dianne Hamilton tapped on her screen as she shouted, "Eric, we're playing it in here!"

"I figured," her husband said, as he rushed into the family room.

The red background on the entertainment screen faded to orange, the star logo shrank, and "Emergency Transmission from VPS *Audace*" appeared in large, bold letters below it. Near the bottom of the screen, in small grey text, read, "C. Brugnaro commanding. Authorization E-3-14: p1, p5."

The screen faded to reveal the head and shoulders of an older individual in dress uniform sitting in front of a gilded version of the SDA star logo.

"This is Captain Massimo Brugnaro commanding officer of the VPS *Audace*," he said formally, "currently assigned to patrol the Harvard Sector under the auspices of the Space Defense Alliance Navy. We are transmitting this emergency broadcast under SDA Code E, Section 3, Chapter 14, Parts 1 and 5.

"Forty-seven days ago, Prosperity Station was destroyed, along with the local interstellar Portal. There were no survivors.

"The radiation levels in the debris field are extremely high, and this ship does not possess suitable equipment to recover your Doors. A properly equipped scout ship has been dispatched from Terra Delta but, due to the destruction of the local Portal, is not expected to arrive for approximately ten months. We regret to inform you that we will not be able to provide any direct assistance until that time.

"Please upload your current status in compliance with Code S, Chapter 97, Part 16 when you activate your emergency beacons. All single-Door stations and any vessel meeting the criteria in SDA Code S, Chapter 97, Part 17 should set their beacon to mayday at this time. When recovery commences, priority will be given to these Doors. Improper beacon use will be subject to prosecution under SDA Code S, Chapter 97, Part 17, Subsection A.

"Since direct two-way communication is not currently possible, SDA Code S, Chapter 97, Part 18 authorizes you to bundle personal messages along with your status reports. These will be routed through our home base in Genoa on Venice, then on to civilian channels. We are also authorized to transmit the SDA sector news feed via a sub-channel so that you can follow current events.

"Current guidance is that any vessel capable of travel immediately set course for the nearest port at best speed. There will be at least one SDA ship stationed in this system at all times until recovery is completed.

"On a personal note," he said, leaning forward, "our thoughts are with you during this trying time, and I have been assured that the SDA will continue searching for ways to assist you. Stay strong. You can get through this.

"Massimo Brugnaro, Captain, VPS *Audace* signing off."

"I'm switching to the news," Dianne said, to fill the silence that followed.

She tapped at her screen, and headlines started scrolling up the entertainment screen as the feed loaded:

Prosperity Station Portal Goes Offline Without Warning

Report of "Major Incident" was Final Message Received from Prosperity Station

Unvarnished Truth Host Calls Prosperity Incident "Obvious PR Stunt"

Owners Report all Prosperity Station Doors Offline

Prosperity Ginhard Implements Continuity of Leadership Plan During Outage

Prosperity Reassures that Connections Will be Restored, Deliveries Will Continue

Reunite Humanity Claims Responsibility for Prosperity Station Attack

Violette was the first to react. "I *told* you that those terrorists were going to cause problems!"

"Don't be absurd," Dianne said, as she struggled to absorb the updates. "There aren't any actual terrorists. It must have been some sort of industrial accident!"

"What kind of *industrial accident* could destroy the station *and the Portal?!*"

"I'm just saying that we don't have all the facts and can't just jump to conclusions," Dianne said, with a slight tremor in her voice. "Director Chaplin warned us about these so-called terrorists. They're just an extremist propaganda tool designed to sow uncertainty before the election."

"The zone director is a puppet who only says what Prosperity tells him to say," Violette retorted angrily.

"I hate it when you get like this!" Dianne said with heat. "You act like Prosperity is some big evil empire, always forgetting that *I work for them.* Do you really think so little of me that you believe I'd work for them if I truly thought they were as bad as you like to make them out to be?!"

"Ugh, you're just parroting the company line! *Everyone* knows what the corporations get up to—"

Dianne angrily interrupted. "And you're just guilelessly accepting the worst conspiracy theory available to reinforce your teen angst!"

"A *good* corporation is the *real* conspiracy theory!"

"Please, both of you calm down and stop for a second," Eric said loudly. "No one knows the answer yet, and the truth is never found in the extreme. Remember that conspiracy theorists, *on either side*, all have one thing in common: the need to be recognized as so much smarter than everyone else that they, and only they, are able to identify the real threats to society. They're not working off facts; they're just stroking their own egos! Now, let's put *our* egos *and* our anxiety aside and stick with what we *actually know!*"

Dianne and Violette looked at each other angrily, but their anger quickly faded.

"Sorry," they said together.

Eric sighed. "Looks like we'll have plenty to talk about at dinner tonight."

The entertainment screen, unseen by the family, continued the scroll of headlines:

Reunite Humanity Blames Portal Technology for Societal Disconnection

Sources Indicate Threats to Prosperity Station Identified 18 Months Before Incident

SDA Rep Denies "Unfounded" Attack Claims

Insider Confirms Prosperity Station Portal Destroyed

Without Portal, Help Won't Arrive at Prosperity Station for Two Months

Prosperity CEO Arrives on Ginhard, Will Brief Press "Soon"

Sources Report Lax Enforcement of Emergency Supply Regulations

Experts Warn That Half of "On the Stars" Residents Could Die Before Help Arrives

Prosperity CEO Brian Masters Declares "No Evidence" of Additional Threats

Quantum Tunnel Disruption Blamed for Prosperity Station Portal Loss

Prosperity Negligence Suits Claim CEO "Fled" Station Before Attack

Unvarnished Truth Host Claims PR Stunt Quote was "Taken Out of Context"

Reunite Humanity Threatens to Eliminate all Portal Factories

CHAPTER FOURTEEN

After a little over two days of hyperspeed travel, the PCV *Faro* shuttle 1's reserves dropped below its minimal power threshold, and it automatically engaged emergency protocols.

Captain Alvin Faro, fully aware that the powered portion of his voyage was nearing its end, was waiting on the bridge when the emergency alert started buzzing.

As part of the safe navigation protocol, the shuttle positioned itself safely just outside of the shipping lane before dropping its spacial distortion field and firing its forward thrusters to bring itself to a complete stop.

Alvin looked over the instructions he had programmed one last time before tapping the **SUBMIT** button.

The console objected with a loud buzz.

"One last hope," Alvin told himself, as he overrode the objection, pointed the shuttle back into the shipping lane, and locked the engines on full.

"Well, Maria, that's it," he said sadly a few minutes later, when the shuttle's power levels dropped too low to maintain thrust and the engines died.

"Every little bit helps," he muttered to himself, as he flicked off the **POWER** switch.

He rose and left the now darkened bridge and, as the door slid closed, added, "Now we wait and hope for a patrol."

The rest of the shuttle was as dark as the bridge, with the exception of a single dimly lit panel just above his head. As he moved along, the ship turned panels on and off to maintain that single column of light around him.

Alvin, and his column of illumination, moved slowly to the far side of the table where he sat down in front of a nearly cold meal.

"Well, Maria," he said, picking up his utensils, "it's a good thing I printed a few extra meals. It will give us time to figure out what to do next."

He started eating but, after just a few forkfuls, paused and declared, "Still going, Maria, onward and upward until the bitter end!"

After finishing his meal, the column of light followed him into the kitchen where he dropped the plate, cup, and utensils into the now disabled recycle chute. It continued following him to the narrow fold-down bunk at the rear of the shuttle where he spent his nights.

"Good night, Maria," Alvin said, as he settled down on the bunk and pulled the blanket over himself. "Lights!"

Alvin and the column of light retired to rest.

After two days, Alvin finished the last of his pre-printed meals and finally resigned himself to working out a next step.

"Well, Maria," he said, as he gathered the last of his supplies on the counter in front of the shuttle's basic, and now useless, printer, "we've still got a few bottles of water and plenty of cartridges."

He paused in thought, finally picking up a cartridge labeled 'oat.' "All the printer *really* does is heat and hydrate. Maybe I can be my own printer."

Alvin retrieved a rarely-used mixing bowl from a cabinet, set it on the counter, then opened several drawers until he found one containing a large, serrated knife. Pressing the cartridge down on the counter with his left hand, he spent several minutes awkwardly sawing off the top of it with the knife.

"There *has* to be a better way to do that," he said breathlessly, as he dumped the newly freed contents into the mixing bowl.

He examined the contents of the bowl—a heap of fine grey powder. "Well, Maria, isn't that appetizing?"

After picking out a few shards of the cartridge, Alvin shook the bowl back and forth until the concentrated oat powder settled into a smooth, flat surface. He used his finger to draw a smiley face, paused to admire his work, then picked up a half-full bottle of water. "Don't want to use it all, just enough to make it edible."

He carefully poured a little bit into the smiling mouth, then stirred the now damp powder, adding more water, a tiny bit at a time, until the power became a thick paste.

He scooped up a large glob with two fingers and quickly stuck it into his mouth.

After an involuntary gag, he forced the unpleasant porridge down. "That's pretty bad." He coughed and took a swig of water. "I might as well eat it directly out of the cartridge."

Another two days later, still silhouetted by his personal column of light but now also wrapped with a thick blanket to ward off the growing cold, Alvin shuffled slowly through the shuttle.

He didn't even register the constant buzzing of the emergency alarm, which he had never bothered to disable, instead focusing on the scraping sound of his slippers against the floor.

He fished out a random cartridge from a pile on the counter, then picked up a multi-driver from nearby. Without even glancing at the cartridge's label, he set it down, then struck the cartridge as hard as he could. The casing dented, so he hit it again and again until it finally cracked enough to allow him to pry it open with the other end of the tool.

He poured the powdery contents into his mouth and washed it down with a swig from the last bottle of potable water and a grimace.

"Well, Maria," he said, wiping away a few particles of powder clinging to his cracked lips, "your cooking sure has gone downhill lately."

He chuckled darkly as he began his slow return to his bunk.

Later that evening, the loud buzzing finally stopped, and the already dim light faded away entirely. Alvin sighed with relief and pulled his blanket tighter around himself.

"Good night, my love. I'll see you soon."

CHAPTER FIFTEEN

Captain Bud was not accustomed to being actively disliked or to having someone hold him responsible for things that *weren't even his fault*. However, he was equally unaccustomed to giving up.

His philosophy, which had been established late in his pampered childhood, was that there was always a way to put the chill back into any situation, no matter how bad, you just had to keep looking until you found it.

After much soul searching, he now felt that, despite his earlier setbacks, he finally had that solution. He was confident that, this time, he would get life on the ship back to normal, back to the way it should be.

As soon as he saw his shipmate the next morning, he stood up straight and started with step one.

"I apologize for how I've been treating you," he said, in his most sincere tone. "This situation has been getting to me much more than I've been able to admit to myself, and I took it out on you. I'm truly sorry and hope that we can try a fresh start."

"Don't forget what happened the last time you tried to get *fresh!*" Ariel replied, with a dubious glare and a raised fist.

"No, no, of course not," he said, putting a hand over his heart. "That's behind us now, and I've learned my lesson. You have my word on that."

Captain Bud smiled and pulled a meal kit from his pocket.

"I found some breakfast kits stuck all the way in the back of the storage area yesterday and thought they might be a small step towards making up for my bad behavior."

With a flourish, he spun the cartridge around so that she could read the label. "Buttermilk pancakes with margarine and maple syrup."

"Wow," Ariel said, with genuine pleasure, resisting the urge to make a grab for the cartridge before her unstable host changed his mind. "A *real* breakfast!?"

"Yes," Captain Bud said, nodding eagerly, "and I'm saving them all for you. I'm totally fine with fries. Just take a seat at the table when you're ready, and I'll get it started for you. Make sure you use the blue chair; it's the most comfortable."

A few minutes later, he returned from the kitchen with a steaming plate of food and placed it in front of her with great fanfare.

She ignored him and quickly started cutting into the pancakes. They were slightly stale, the kit being well past its best by date, but the margarine and warm maple syrup were more than enough to compensate.

After a few frantic mouthfuls, Ariel calmed herself, then forced herself to slow down and take the time to savor the rest of the meal.

She was interrupted periodically by Captain Bud inquiring whether there was anything else she needed. At her negative response he, wisely, retreated and allowed her to enjoy her meal in peace.

Although lunch was the same burger and chili fries that made up the vast majority of their meals aboard the *Rockhard*, it was surprisingly pleasant; Captain Bud was polite, civil, and apologetic. In another complete reversal, he even listened with apparent interest whenever she spoke.

Over an equally civil dinner, Captain Bud preempted their usual conflict and insisted that Ariel take the bedroom for the night.

The evening grew late and Ariel, relaxed for the first time since becoming trapped aboard the *Rockhard*, headed to bed.

Captain Bud felt a rush of long-awaited vindication when there was no click to secure the door behind her.

"That worked faster than I expected," he said gleefully, as he rushed into the bathroom to prepare.

Twenty minutes later, his hair and naked body glistening, Captain Bud moved eagerly from the bathroom to the bedroom.

The room was dark, presumably to avoid any awkward and unnecessary discussion about how unfair she had been treating him.

His entire body pounding with anticipation, he carefully slid under the silk sheets and, with a profound sense of relief, snuggled up against his, finally back to her senses, companion's warm back. He gently wrapped his arms around her, rested his hands on her belly, and started softly kissing her shoulder.

As Captain Bud began to slide his hands upwards, his ears registered a loud noise, but he was far too focused on the successful completion of his plan for any other part of him to take note.

Unexpectedly, something struck him in the face, and the warm back disappeared.

"Lights!" a voice in the distance shouted.

Captain Bud sat up in confusion, shielding his eyes from the new and unwelcome illumination. "Hey, what…?"

The antique lamp that his mother had given him the day he had christened the *Rockhard* struck him hard in his already unpleasantly throbbing face.

As he wiped blood from his eyes, Captain Bud saw his companion standing at the side of the bed in the blue pajamas that they had printed the day they had been disconnected from the station.

As he wondered how she had gotten dressed so quickly, he noticed how red her face was. Perhaps she was choking! He moved towards her to help.

"What the hell is wrong with you?!" She grabbed his nightstand and lifted it into the air. The drawer slid out and fell to the floor, its contents scattering around the room. "If you get any closer, I'll bash your head in!"

Despite the situation, Captain Bud couldn't help noticing how impressive her chest was beneath the thin fabric of her pajama top when it heaved like it was at just that moment.

"I don't understand." He paused in surprise as he tasted blood and finally started to notice just how much of it was dripping down onto his chest. He set the realization aside and continued with more important matters. "The door wasn't locked. I thought—"

"Get it through your thick skull that you and I are *never* going to share 'intimate time' *ever again!*"

Captain Bud was stunned. "But—"

"But nothing!" She brandished the nightstand over her shoulder like a weapon. *"Get out!"*

Taking the better part of valor, Captain Bud complied.

Ariel shouted after him as he retreated towards the door, "And if you *ever* try something like that again, I will break both your legs, *just for fun*, before I throw you out the airlock!"

His face grey with defeat, Captain Bud glanced back into the room for one last glimpse before the door closed behind him.

Ariel threw the nightstand into the far corner of the room where it, disappointingly, didn't even scratch the on-trend wallpaper but at least had the decency to shed a leg, which bounced towards the center of the room.

She moved quickly to the door, locked it, and shuddered.

CHAPTER SIXTEEN

The PCV *Hamilton*'s cargo elevator rattled to a halt, and the doors slid open.

"Violette, are you down here?" Eric Hamilton said, as he stepped into the cargo hold.

"I'll be right there," her voice responded from the far end of the hold.

Eric started walking to meet his daughter halfway.

"Before you get mad…" Violette said from behind him.

"Sagged!" he responded in alarm, spinning around to face her. "You didn't!"

Behind her in the corner was an active Door leaning against the wall. A green extension cord stretched from a wall outlet to the lower left-hand corner of the Door frame, and four irregular pieces of packing material were stuffed into the clamp sockets.

"I just needed to feel like I was *going* somewhere!" Violette pleaded.

"Your mother is going to flip out." Eric stepped closer to the Door. "You know we're responsible for delivering these *exactly as we received them!*"

"Hey, at least I didn't toss another Door through it." She gestured towards the stacks of packaged doors that filled the hold. "I've always wanted to see how far it would get before the tunnels collapse."

"That's not helpful…" He paused to groan as he noticed the Door's gold label. "And, of course, you opened one of the deluxe sets. Just one of the ZPGs in those costs more than our entire Door set did!"

"Yeah, sorry," Violette grabbed onto his arm, "but I stayed away from the yellow-labels!"

"Thanks, your mother will appreciate that," he replied insincerely, then rubbed his temples for a moment. "The way things are, opening one of the custom configurations would probably be less of an issue. I doubt that they'll ever get where they were going."

"If they do," Violette said, forcing a smile, "they'll arrive *exactly as we received them.*"

Her father groaned again. "You'd better let me do the talking when we tell your mother, *and* you'd better expect to work off the fine."

"Well," Violette said thoughtfully, "I haven't been receiving my allowance lately, so maybe we can put that towards the fine."

"That's not how this works," her father replied, with a severe look.

"A girl can hope," she said, with a weak grin.

"Come on," Eric said, refusing to acknowledge her attempt to lighten the mood. "We need to let your mother know what's happened to her cargo."

Dianne Hamilton was reviewing the latest news reports in her office within the family work suite.

Things back with the rest of humanity were getting worse, and she could feel her anxiety bubbling in her stomach.

She looked up from the large screen on her desk as she heard her husband and daughter coming down the hall. Surely some family time would lift her spirits.

That hope faded when she saw her husband's firm expression and her daughter's guilty one.

She looked inquiringly at her daughter. "How could you have gotten into trouble when we can't even go anywhere?"

Unnoticed even by himself, Eric flinched at the comment.

Violette, hoping to steer the conversation in the best possible direction, said, "It's really not that big—"

"She opened one of the deluxe Door sets," Eric said, "and set them up in the cargo container."

Violette looked up at her father with a frown.

Dianne shut her eyes. "Should I even ask why?"

"We've just been so cooped up—" Violette started.

"Nostalgia," Eric interrupted harshly. "She said she wanted to feel like she was *going* somewhere."

Dianne looked at her daughter, who didn't meet her gaze. "Do you know how expensive those are?"

"Just one of the ZPGs costs more—" Violette started seriously.

"Rhetorical question," Dianne said with frustration. "We have an obligation—"

"To deliver them *exactly as we receive them*, I know," Violette quoted, before her mother could finish.

The room went silent.

"I really can't deal with this right now," Dianne said, then pointed diagonally across the hall. "Go to your room, and we'll discuss this at dinner."

Violette opened her mouth to argue but saw the look on her mother's face, quickly reconsidered, then fled.

"There's something else wrong, isn't there?" Eric asked, as the door to Violette's bedroom closed.

"Several things. Pull up a chair."

Eric reached into his own office beside hers, grabbed his chair, dragged it into the doorway, and sat down.

"There have been two more attacks," she started sadly. "Andersen Portal Systems managed to protect their Portal, but Jantal was a complete loss, just like Prosperity."

"So," Eric replied quietly, "not an isolated incident then."

"No." Dianne went quiet again.

"And…" Eric prompted.

"Prosperity has filed."

"Crap."

"It might not be so bad," she said, placing her hand on his knee. "They'll probably invoke the contract cancellation clause, so we would be able to sell our cargo."

"Then why don't you sound more optimistic?"

"Prosperity is, *was*, the only agent on Ginhard. There's no telling how long it will take for the office to get sold off and reopened, so we'll have to head right back out to another system to find someone we could sell them to."

"Can we manage that?"

"I think so." She rubbed her hands against her eyes. "Since we have no other income anymore, we'd run through pretty much all of our savings, but we should have enough to cover one more trip."

"No wonder you're looking glum."

"It's not all bad news," she said, forcing a reassuring smile. "After the second attack, the SDA government passed an emergency support resolution for those of us affected."

"Are they offering enough to cover the second trip?"

"I don't know." She leaned back in her chair. "No one does. They're still working out the mechanics of who gets what. All the post said was that vessels like ours would get to choose between a financial transfer or a supply drop."

"I wouldn't say no to either."

"Yeah," she replied, with a pained look, "but let's stop taking about it right now."

"Let me fix you something to eat, then we can figure out what to do about Violette's trip."

"Oh, that girl!"

"She reminds me of you."

"Don't even start!"

CHAPTER SEVENTEEN

Captain Pamela Orbison was a year away from retirement and dreading its arrival.

After her husband's passing ten years before, she had thrown herself into her work as captain of the ΔPS *Steadfast*. She had been so successful that, for the middle five of those years, she had aggressively fended off annual offers of promotion. Her final refusal, a tense shouting match where she had spat on the very idea of being stuck planet- or station-side, had been convincing but had also left her very much in the bad graces of command.

Her current assignment was to local system patrol in the Ginhard system within the backwater Harvard sector. Prior to her arrival, her entire knowledge of the sector had been limited to its inclusion in the list of First Wave sectors from human history class.

While she chafed at the limited mobility of system duty, she was content to remain in command of a ship.

She was surprised and apprehensive when her virtual assistant, currently configured as a pulsing ball of green light, interrupted her morning ritual with an urgent summons from the system commander.

"Reserve a priority lift!" she ordered the sphere, as she quickly threw on her dress uniform and rushed from the room.

A few moments later, the priority lift deposited her and she ran into the *Steadfast*'s shore room just around the corner from the lift lobby, which contained the ship's two Doors. Nodding to the officer on duty, she slapped the Pad on the local Door and stepped through to the Ginhard System Command station. Once there, she followed tapping prompts from her wristband, which guided her along a pre-authorized route to the Commodore's office.

By the time she lowered herself into the closest of the two guest chairs, she had hidden her nervousness behind a professionally calm expression.

Commodore Mariam Tateossian, commander of the HG Fleet stationed at Ginhard, scrutinized her for a moment before tapping on her screen.

"I'll get straight to the point," Commodore Tateossian said, as she folded her hands on the desk in front of her. "We're dispatching *Steadfast* on a rescue and recovery flight."

Captain Orbison was surprised. *Steadfast* was the last ship in the system after 京SS *Xi'an* had been equipped with a long-range ZPG sled and sent to reestablish communications with the Romanov Commune station after it was disconnected by the Prosperity Incident.

Noticing, or at least anticipating, Orbison's reaction, the commodore added, "BSS *Natick* will be arriving through the Portal within the hour to cover your station."

Orbison nodded. "Where are we bound, sir?"

"Along the Prosperity shipping lane. The PCV *Faro* has been out of contact since the incident and has now missed its scheduled delivery date. Normally we wouldn't dispatch a ship for a vessel that is only two weeks overdue, but these are not normal times, and we have received reports that the captain is a recent widower. There is concern that, with no one else aboard, he may become self-destructive in isolation.

"Complicating matters is the fact that we've also been notified that they are redirecting a new Portal to the former site of Prosperity Station to facilitate the recovery process and that it will be coming through Ginhard in the next few weeks. It is imperative that the lane is clear before that transport arrives.

"Non-portable recovery supplies will be delivered by the end of the day, and you are ordered to depart immediately upon receipt. Command has also dispatched JSS *Vancouver* and assigned it to the remaining ZPG sled to provide long-range support while you are on mission.

"You are ordered to locate the *Faro*, recover its captain, and verify that it has followed safe navigation protocols and is not a navigational hazard. Then continue on to the former site of Prosperity Station, clearing any other navigational hazards that you encounter."

As Captain Orbison followed the taps from her wristband back to the correct Door, she had time to reflect on the story of the widower captain. It hit her hard. She found it all too easy to remember what life had been like for her immediately after her husband's passing. The idea of going through that completely alone was horrifying.

As she stepped through the Door back to the *Steadfast*, she experienced a rare moment of self-honesty and realized that she had been fleeing the pain from that loss ever since.

Her executive officer, Commander Obelius Frangopoulos, was waiting in the shore room when she arrived but, seeing her distant look, didn't interrupt her thoughts until she finally glanced in his direction. "Orders, sir?"

"Recovery and navigational hazard check on the Prosperity lane. We will be receiving a cargo delivery and are to depart immediately after it has been offloaded."

"Aye, sir. I'll let you know as soon as we're notified of the cargo's arrival time." He nodded and left the room, turning right to head towards the bridge.

Captain Orbison followed but turned left to take the lift back to the officer's residence deck. As the lift made its way upwards, her mind drifted back to her earlier realization and upcoming retirement, and she wondered whether it was finally time to end her self-imposed isolation.

Captain Orbison joined Commander Frangopoulos in the flight deck observation room half an hour later as the cargo shuttle disgorged its load of donations.

"My cousin Grace's work is in there," Frangopoulos said, pointing to the pallet being floated off the shuttle.

Captain Orbison turned to him in surprise. "I heard that Cogswell made a big donation, but I thought it was just Conduits."

"It was," Commander Frangopoulos said, nodding. "But she was promoted to final assembly on the Conduit line a few months ago, and her team was assigned to prep Cogswell's donations."

"Pass along my congratulations."

The XO laughed. "I will, and I'm sure she'll be just as thrilled with them as she was with mine."

"Oh to be that young again," Orbison replied wistfully.

They both watched as the shuttle's cargo door closed and it readied itself for departure.

"I'm surprised they didn't send any Doors," Orbison mused. "It would make things so much easier."

"Still not keeping up with current events, I see," Frangopoulos said with a grin before continuing over his captain's good-natured grimace. "As soon as news about Prosperity Station got out there was a rush on Doors and the prices went through the roof. Even if someone was willing to put up the cost, I doubt they could find any."

"I suppose it would be hard to donate something you don't have."

Frangopoulos turned serious. "What do you think the chances are this will end up being a rescue?"

Captain Orbison grimaced again. "I don't even want to entertain the other option."

CHAPTER EIGHTEEN

Captain Bud was depressed and tired of the angry routine that had taken over the *Rockhard*. This was *not* what things were supposed to be like, and it was *not* what he expected out of life.

They were still two weeks away from the edge of the zone and an end to his ordeal. His depression was getting so bad that he could barely breathe.

Although it was a struggle, he still maintained hope that he could somehow figure out a return to normalcy with his companion. Unfortunately, his most recent attempt at civil conversation had quickly resulted in unfounded accusations that he was fouling the very air around them. He hadn't come up with anything better but knew it would come to him eventually—it always did. He splashed water on his face and steeled himself for the day, confident that at least things couldn't possibly get worse.

While stepping out of the bathroom, Captain Bud suddenly realized that it had been more than a week since he had been on the bridge. This was surprising because, before things had gone downhill, he had always looked forward to spending time on the bridge, the nerve center of *his* ship. He had often visited several times in a single day just to review the usually unchanged status board and soak in the atmosphere of the room.

He leisurely walked to the bridge, studiously ignoring the angry eyes that followed him from the table where his companion was having breakfast.

With the door to the bridge safely locked behind him, he settled into the command chair with a sigh of contentment.

After a few minutes of savoring the moment, he activated the controls and realized with dismay that *quite a lot* had changed in the past week. Several status indicators had turned red, and one of them was even flashing.

Captain Bud's heart nearly stopped when he saw that the flashing indicator was labeled **LIFE SUPPORT**, and it practically leapt from his chest when he saw that one of the other ones was the one labeled **POWER**.

"Power status," he said, after a long moment of indecision.

A status window expanded out of the **POWER** indicator. At the top of the window was a bold red warning:

Flare detected in primary Zero-Point Generator

No alternate power sources configured

Immediate load reduction required.

Below the warning was an analog-style gauge displaying the Zero-Point Generator's current load level. The needle was pointing to 74%, just under the midpoint of the red danger zone.

"Activate power save mode," Captain Bud ordered, with a quavering voice. "Discontinue the diagnostic scans on the Door and Conduit. Reduce cabin lighting to 80%, and shut off all cabin screens except main entertainment. Cut power to B deck, docking, and all bridge systems except this console."

The entire room changed, taking on an unadorned grey appearance.

The needle dropped to 52%.

Captain Bud sighed. "Disable *all* holographic projectors."

In the bedroom, the intricate scrollwork trimming the ceiling flattened, while the hardwood flooring and trendy wallpaper all faded to reveal their unfashionably grey reality.

The needle dropped out of the red to land at 47%.

"Whew, that could have been bad. Back."

The status window retreated into the **POWER** indicator, which was now green.

Captain Bud took a deep breath to steady himself, closed his eyes for a moment, then, fighting back nearly overwhelming trepidation, ended his procrastination. "Life support status."

A new window expanded, this time from the flashing indicator, and was quickly covered by five copies of a bold, flashing message in large red text reading,

Atmospheric filter impedance has exceeded operational parameters

Immediate replacement required

"Oh," he said anxiously. "Alice isn't going to like this *at all.*"

Captain Bud set his wristband projector to flashlight mode and started down the smooth crawlway along the port cold-wall of the *Rockhard's* lower half-height B deck. The crawlway extended two-thirds of the length of the vessel before making a ninety-degree turn along the partitioned off aft section of the deck.

The remainder of the deck's open area was covered by a rough grey surface, which had been poured in to protect the insulation layer of the hull after the fuel tanks that formerly occupied the space had been removed. Cases of chili fries were stacked neatly near the bridge, and a variety of boxes and old personal possessions were gathered haphazardly against the opposite starboard cold-wall. In the middle of the deck was a large number of partially crushed boxes, all labeled "Emergency Supplies," which Captain Bud had been using to work out his frustrations during the increasingly difficult voyage.

At the end of the crawlway's inward section was an entryway to the engine and life support access room. It was small, with only enough room for two people to stand shoulder-to-shoulder, but unlike the rest of the deck, it was tall enough to allow them to stand. The extra height was due to the fact that the lower half of the room extending into the engine pod attached to the bottom of the vessel. Across the top of the opening to the room was a chin-up bar that was used to lift oneself back up onto the crawlway.

Inside the room were three small access ways: two on the fore and aft walls of the lower half of the room that gave access to the engine pod's inner workings, and one on the upper half of the aft wall that led into the environmental systems behind the aft wall. The upper half of the room's fore wall was covered by a set of doors labeled "Power Control," and the entire remaining wall was covered by a set of doors labeled "Environmental Control."

Captain Bud opened the larger environmental control doors and stepped back involuntarily as a noxious stench escaped from it. He nearly toppled backwards onto the crawlway when his rump struck its raised ledge.

Stepping forward again, he grabbed a yellow handle along the right edge of the open environmental access and pulled out the ship's atmosphere filter.

There was a loud squeal, and a screen built into the back of the left-side door lit up and displayed:

Filter removed - environmental systems offline

Captain Bud set the filter on the floor between his bare feet, directly on top of a large grate that covered the recycle drain, then stretched up and pulled a hose down through a roughly cut opening in the ceiling.

The hose was tipped with a sprayer attachment, and he spent a few minutes spraying the filter with it. After the filter slowly changed from black to dark grey, he shook it dry and inserted it back into the wall.

The screen changed to read:

Replacement filter detected - environmental systems online

There was another squeal, then the screen changed back to:

Atmospheric filter impedance has exceeded operational parameters

Immediate replacement required

With a groan, Captain Bud pulled the filter out again for another rushed cleaning. He groaned again when he replaced it and was met with the same results.

With resignation, he removed the filter once again and spent ten minutes carefully spraying each side of the filter until the dark grey turned to light grey.

He watched the "replacement filter detected" message anxiously until it finally changed to:

Atmospheric filter impedance is high

Immediate replacement recommended

After pulling himself back up through the access hatch into the bridge and dusting himself off, Captain Bud flopped bonelessly into the command chair. He spent several minutes there with his eyes closed working out the best way to frame this new development to minimize the pain of the upcoming confrontation.

Captain Bud finished his presentation with, "I had to wash out the filter three times before it started up again."

"You *washed* the filter?!" Ariel was so stunned that she barely raised her voice.

"Despite what the manufacturer claims, you don't *really* need to keep replacing them. The dirt must have been why the air was getting stale," Captain Bud answered with confidence that faded as he continued. "I've never any problems before."

"Before?" Ariel rolled her eyes. "You mean back when you were opening your Door every day and letting in fresh air?"

"I suppose…" Captain Bud admitted in a small voice.

With resignation and painful foreknowledge, Ariel asked, "Why don't you *replace* the filter?"

"Uh," Captain Bud squirmed in anticipation of her angry response, "I don't have one to replace it with."

Ariel sighed and, feeling a macabre obligation to finish the line of inquiry, softly asked, "Why not?"

Caught by surprise he answered truthfully. "Why would I pay for a *new* filter when I can just *reuse* the one that I already have?"

Ariel put her head in her hands but said nothing.

Uncomfortable with her uncharacteristically subdued response, Captain Bud felt compelled to offer reassurance. "On the plus side, now that we have a documented emergency, the SOS is broadcasting, and I got the power load down below 50% so the generator shouldn't degrade any further."

"That's good to hear," Ariel responded, lifting her head to reveal an evil grin. "Now, when life support gives out, at least I'll be able to watch you die."

After that, Captain Bud gave up the nightly struggle over possession of the bedroom and started sleeping exclusively on the locked bridge.

CHAPTER NINETEEN

Dianne Hamilton's wristband lit up red. She tapped it, and a gravelly voice said, "ΔPS *Steadfast* to unidentified vessel, you are ordered to transmit your identification codes pursuant to SDA Code S, Chapter 1, Part 3."

Her mother swiped downwards along her wristband and a control panel projected onto her forearm. She swiped a few times, then made several taps.

"ΔPS *Steadfast*," she said, "this is Captain Dianne Hamilton of the PCV *Hamilton*. I have activated our Identification beacon."

"Confirmed, *Hamilton*. Have you encountered any other vessels since departing Prosperity Station?"

"Negative, *Steadfast*. We've had no contacts since the incident."

"Acknowledged, *Hamilton*. PCV *Faro* is overdue, and we have been dispatched to investigate. Please transmit your object detection logs."

"Do they mean old man Faro?" Violette asked her father anxiously. Eric shushed her and nodded.

"Affirmative, *Steadfast*," Dianne responded, and after a few more taps on her arm, "Transmitting now. We haven't had any proximity alarms, so the data has not been reviewed."

"Acknowledged, *Hamilton*, transmission received. Thank you for your assistance." The voice paused. "What is your vessel status? Do you have enough supplies to make it to port safely?"

"Affirmative, *Steadfast*," more taps, "broadcasting our status packet now."

"Received, *Hamilton*." The voice from the other ship paused again. "According to your packet, provision levels are marginal, at best."

She sighed. "Affirmative, *Steadfast*. We're a bit thinner than launch and getting tired of protein bars, but our calculations indicate that we'll just make it."

"Acknowledged, *Hamilton*." The voice paused again, another voice was nearly audible in the background. "We were deployed as a rescue flight, and our captain has just authorized an emergency supply drop for your vessel. We will deploy an unmanned pod at closest point of approach. It will be stocked with provisions and a Conduit connected with Ginhard."

The room exploded in cheers, the volume far exceeding what you would expect from three tired and slightly undernourished voices.

"Acknowledged, *Steadfast*." Dianne choked back tears as her daughter grabbed her husband's hands and started dancing him around in a circle. "It will be nice to be connected to civilization again."

"Good luck, *Hamilton*. I'm connecting you to our quartermaster to arrange the transfer."

The *Hamilton*'s docking area was positioned at the very back of the vessel behind the second set of double doors in the storeroom. The docking area had three sections: two extending arms, one on either side intended for connecting to larger craft, and a fixed central port for pods and transfer shuttles. Extending beyond the docking area was the main bulk of the cargo container attached to the bottom of the vessel between the two engine pods.

It was just after lunch when *Steadfast* pod 19 settled against the central docking port. After a melody of clunks and hisses as the *Hamilton* took hold of the pod, the light to the left side of the docking hatch turned green.

"Finally!" Violette shouted, yanking open the hatch. "Real food and civilized data!"

She grabbed the handle on the pod's corresponding hatch and tried to twist it, but it wouldn't budge.

"The code, Violette," her father reminded her calmly.

"Oh, yeah, duh!" She stood up straight and loudly recited, "Access Code E S 5 7 6 D."

There was a click from inside the hatch.

Her second attempt succeeded, and the handle twisted. She pulled the hatch open to reveal a cramped and poorly lit space filled with clear plastic boxes stacked awkwardly on and around the single control seat, which had been spun around backwards to face the hatch.

"I see the Conduit!" Violette shouted, pointing at a blue cylinder visible through the side of a box wedged against the ceiling towards the back of the pile.

"And I see vegetables," her father said excitedly, while reaching past his daughter to release the closest strap holding the boxes in place.

It took a few minutes to release the remainder of the straps and several additional moments to stop the boxes from tumbling out on their own.

There were six boxes in total: one filled with fresh vegetables; one with a selection of vat-grown meats and fish; three with a selection of non-perishable food cartridges; and the final box, which contained the Conduit and a variety of other items.

The Conduit box had a note printed on Samaritan Charity Services letterhead, which was stuck to the inside of the cover so that it could be read through it:

Please accept this small contribution and know that our thoughts are with you during this difficult time.

The enclosed items were all provided through the generous donations of companies and individuals moved by your plight.

It is our hope that these tokens will help maintain your spirits and keep you going.

Dianne placed the donations on top of the rest of the boxes on the cargo cart that usually resided on the shuttle deck.

As Eric took the cart's handle, Violette's anticipation overwhelmed her and she lunged forward, yanked off the lid and dug down the side of the box to grab the Conduit.

The blue Conduit was capped with translucent plastic on both ends and had a slightly crooked sticker on the side reading:

Courtesy of Cogswell Conduits: one-year free unlimited basic access
Doing our small part to help you through this difficult time.

"Civilization!" she shouted, holding it up high like a torch.

"I'll take that." Her mother snatched it away and slipped it into a pocket in her overalls. "I'll install it as soon as we finish unpacking these boxes."

"Aw," Violette started, before her eyes caught sight of something else in the box.

She lunged in again and fished out two data chips. One was marked "Peacock Entertainment—six-month decryption key" and the other "Stream Five Productions—one-year decryption key."

"*Yes!* Stream Five has all the best matches!" She quickly stuffed them into her own pocket to avoid a repeat of the loss of the Conduit. "I'm going to load this up as soon as we're connected!"

Giving in to Violette's excitement, her father reached past her and pulled out a book. "My dad used to collect these!"

Violette pulled out two more. "*Printed* books!" she cried, hugging them to her chest. "I feel so *fancy!*"

Her reaction to a grey box with a control panel on top was not as enthusiastic. She picked it up and held it out to her parents.

"A holo-emitter? Isn't this the same brand that Grandma used?"

"Violette…" her father started.

"I see some more chips under the board games!" She excitedly interrupted her father by tossing the projector into his unprepared arms. "Oooh!" she said, pulling out a black box. "Ice cream cartridges!"

"I'll take those." Her father grabbed the box from her hands. "We know you hate the stuff that comes out of our printer, and ice cream is so *untextured!*"

"I'll make an exception!" Violette laughed, making several half-hearted attempts to get them back. "I'll even say I was *wrong!*" She paused. "I wasn't, of course, but I'd *gladly* lie for ice cream!"

Later that afternoon, after the boxes had been unloaded and, at Dianne's insistence, properly logged, she took the new Conduit into the foyer. With the family watching, she removed all the old Conduits, except for the emergency receiver, and handed them to Eric who stuffed them into the closest cabinet. She handed the Cogswell Conduit to Violette and pointed to the now vacant socket beneath the emergency receiver.

"Why don't you do the honors."

Violette inserted the Conduit and, with exaggerated caution, twisted it until it locked into place.

She stepped back, and they all watched the flashing yellow light until it turned green—glowing proof that a small piece of normalcy had been recovered.

Nearly an hour later, Dianne poked her head into her husband's office.

"I finally finished going through my messages," she said, as she stepped fully into the doorway. "We got one from the guild; as expected, Prosperity has terminated all outstanding shipping contracts as part of their bankruptcy proceedings."

"Now that it's official, what does that mean for us?" Eric asked, while closing a paused message from one of his now former coworkers who had also survived the incident.

"Most immediately," she replied, leaning against the door frame, "it means that there won't be a delivery fee waiting for us at Ginhard."

There was cheering from down the hall as Violette celebrated her team's victory.

"That's okay," he replied with a nod. "We expected that. We should have enough in savings—"

"That's another thing." Dianne shook her head. "Our bank's HQ was on the station, and they had billions in loans out to Prosperity, so they've gone under, too. All accounts are frozen." At her husband's downcast look, she added, "Fortunately, we never transferred our shipping fee out of the guild account..."

"Why the glum face?" Violette asked, squeezing into the doorway beside her mother.

"Prosperity terminated our contract," her mother answered.

"Wait," Violette said, excited. "Doesn't that mean that the Doors are *ours* now? They're worth a *fortune!* People will be lining up to buy them from us!"

"It's not that simple," her mother replied, putting an arm around her daughter. "They've been classified as salvage—we can't sell them to just anyone, only an authorized recovery agent. If we got caught trying to sell them ourselves, we would forfeit the entire claim and end up with nothing."

"What if we just don't get caught?"

Dianne controlled her response, hoping her daughter wasn't being completely serious. "You know that's not how we do things."

"I know, but it doesn't seem *fair!*" Violette protested, looking to her father for support.

"It was designed to prevent profiteering and disruption of the distribution chain during a financial crisis," her father explained.

"Okay, we're connected again. Just call an *authorized agent* right now!" Violette said eagerly. "They could be waiting for us as soon as we get there!"

"The only authorized agent for Doors on Ginhard was Prosperity," her mother replied, with another shake of her head. "It's always been too close to the station for competitors to risk establishing offices there."

"But..." Violette started.

Her mother quickly thwarted her advice by interjecting, "Before I was so rudely interrupted," she squeezed her daughter's shoulders to take the edge off of her comment, "I was about to tell your father that we're going to have to find some way to fund another outbound trip so that we can get them to another agent. We can't wait who knows how long until the local office is auctioned off or another company sets up shop."

Violette looked so crestfallen that her father took pity on her and offered, "Perhaps it's time for dinner."

She perked up. "Can I pick?!"

"I hate beets!" Eric shouted, lifting a slice of the offending root, which happened to be his daughter's favorite, that he had speared on the end of his fork. "But I've never been happier to eat anything *in my life!*"

He shoved the beet into his mouth with an exaggerated look of ecstasy. The rest of the family laughed but didn't let it distract them from their own salads.

There was a ding from the kitchen.

"Sounds like the 'authentic Pacific genetic stock cod' is ready!" Violette said, wolfing down the last of her salad and leaping up. "I'll get it, and maybe I'll even bring some out for the two of you!"

"Leave mine in the oven," her father instructed. "Unlike *some* people, I'm planning on savoring my meal!"

"Okay," she replied from the kitchen, before starting to sing the word "fish" over and over to herself, the pitch changing with each repetition.

A few minutes later, she came back to the table carrying two plates, each with a rectangular block of fish, some sliced carrots, and a pile of printed rice.

"I don't even care that it's not cut into a proper fish shape!" Violette declared, as she handed one of the plates to her mother.

"I'm not even sure I'd care if it was from a *real* fish!" her father replied, before taking another bite of his salad.

"Don't be gross," Violette said with a grimace, before setting her plate down with exaggerated caution. "I want to enjoy this!"

"Make sure to eat it all!" her mother teased.

"Yeah, fill up!" Eric added. "More ice cream for the rest of us!"

Violette stuck her tongue out at her father, then very delicately cut off a small piece of fish and lifted it towards her mouth. She grinned, aggressively snapped the morsel off her fork, then resumed a muffled version of her fish song as she chewed slowly.

CHAPTER TWENTY

Aboard the ΔPS *Steadfast*, the PCV *Hamilton*'s object detection log was put to immediate use. As soon as it loaded into his workspace, Commander James Lemaître, the *Steadfast*'s Chief Detection Officer, started working with the data.

Since the *Hamilton*'s detection array ranged far beyond the established shipping lane and logged every single mass that it encountered, regardless of size or density, there were millions of entries to sort through. Lemaître filtered the list to solid matter encounters since the Prosperity Station Incident, then sorted the results by size.

He exhaled in relief when he saw that there were only sixteen entries large enough to be the vessel or its shuttle and that only four of those entries had mass readings indicating that they could be hollow.

He exported the four potentials then, following standard recovery protocols, filtered the list to objects that could be a spaced individual or a survival suit. There was little hope that anyone in a suit could have lasted this long, so he felt another wave of relief when the resulting recordset came up empty.

Lemaître returned to the four most likely objects and sorted them by distance. He smiled when he saw that the first one was less than a day away.

He sent the records to the bridge, then followed them there to present his report.

Commander Lemaître was back on the bridge the next afternoon in anticipation of the first encounter. "We are coming up on the detected coordinates for object one. It is no longer there."

"Widen scans," Captain Orbison ordered. "It may be drifting."

"We're detecting something in the right mass range," Commander Lemaître reported. "It looks like an asteroid." After a short pause, he said, "Trajectory confirms that the asteroid is object one. Scans indicate that the low mass is due to an extremely porous composition."

"Move on to object two," Captain Orbison ordered with disappointment.

"Sir," Lieutenant Junior Grade Dermot Walsh, the detection officer on duty, reported nearly a week later, "object detection just picked up something just inside the edge of the shipping lane."

"What is it?" Commander Obelius Frangopoulos, the ship's executive officer, replied from the captain's station.

"Main sensors are coming in range momentarily." After a pause, Lieutenant JG Walsh said, "Our scans indicate that it is a small craft, likely a shuttle."

"Can you identify it?" Commander Frangopoulos responded.

"Negative. It is not broadcasting."

Commander Frangopoulos glanced towards the communications station near the front of the bridge. "Any response?"

Ensign Catriona Flett, the communications officer on duty, shook her head in negation. "No, sir, no response to my hails."

"Keep trying," Commander Frangopoulos instructed.

"Trajectory confirms that the craft is object two," Walsh reported a few minutes later. "It may have dropped from hyperspeed unexpectedly. We could be dealing with a catastrophic system failure."

Commander Frangopoulos nodded to Ensign Flett. "Call Captain Orbison to the bridge."

An hour later, the *Steadfast* had matched speed with the shuttle and launched an inspection pod.

"Coming up on it now," Chief Taren Lutz reported from the pod. "Hull markings confirm that it is PCV *Faro* shuttle 1."

The bridge was silent as the pod positioned itself beside the shuttle and the recovery clamps extended to latch onto it. A third arm snaked between the two small crafts and sought out the emergency access plate just forward of the shuttle's main door.

"We're connected, and the shuttle is powering up." Chief Lutz paused. "Downloading logs now."

A moment later, Chief Lutz said, "Accessing log now."

"Status?" Captain Orbison asked hopefully.

Lutz's voice was flat as she replied, "Confirmed as cold and drifting, sir."

CHAPTER TWENTY-ONE

Ariel awoke gasping for breath and desperately trying to remember where she was.

As she became fully conscious, she remembered—still stuck on the *bocked Rockhard* with the *even more* bocked Captain Bud.

The air in the room was thick and still. As she struggled to catch her breath, she couldn't help but wonder whether Captain Bud had finally managed to kill them both.

She closed her eyes as she gathered her strength, and her thoughts drifted back to happier times.

Before her internment on the *Rockhard*, life had been good. At work, she was hearing hints that she could be in line for a promotion any quarter now. And at home, she was enjoying the companionship of three friends who lived with her aboard the PCV *Tanaka*, an old cargo vessel located just inside the Prosperity Corporate Zone almost directly opposite the Portal and far from any other traffic.

Her friend Zen had inherited the *Tanaka* from an uncle and was happy to rent rooms to friends for far below the market rate as long as they were willing to chip in for maintenance costs now and then.

Rather than feeling worn, the old vessel was comfortable and homey, with bright wallpaper and plush furnishings. The spacious layout didn't hurt its positive impression either.

Each of the four bedrooms, located in the forward half of the vessel, were suites containing both a full bathroom and separate workspace. The communal areas, in the rear half of the vessel past the foyer and cargo elevator (which failed as an elevator, having no stops without a cargo container, and was more aptly described as a storage closet with potential), included a well-equipped kitchen surrounded by a large combined L-shaped dining and living area.

As Zen's skills were limited to the ownership side of "owning and operating," the *Tanaka* rarely moved and was constantly at risk of being reclassified as a station. To avoid this, and the associated permanence of location, Zen threw a weekend-long party every few months and invited a cousin who happened to be a commercial pilot along to fly the *Tanaka* a few lightyears out of the zone then back again.

The thought of those parties soured her already dark mood. It had been at the most recent one that she met the host of the ill-fated Linner party that had led her to her current predicament.

Returning to reality, and resisting the urge to just keep her eyes closed and wait for the inevitable, she rolled to the edge of the bed, panting hard, and sat up.

As soon as her feet hit the floor, she felt a vibration pulse through them. The thumping continued irregularly, the vibration making its way up her legs and into her already queasy stomach as she stumbled towards the door. The final thump faded just before she, on her second attempt, got the door unlocked.

There was a whoosh from a vent just above her head, and she felt the air start moving around her again.

Lightheaded and struggling to keep herself upright, she opened the door and stepped out into the corridor.

After a few steps, she heard a commotion and turned towards it. With great surprise, she saw that, for the first time that she could remember, the door to the bridge was wide open, allowing her to look out of the formerly-gilded front windows.

Just as her curiosity started to draw the rest of her in that direction, Captain Bud appeared in the doorway. He was panting, covered with sweat, and had a large black mark on his forehead that ended in a small wound, which was just starting to bleed. He looked uncharacteristically concerned as he continued into the corridor and closed the door behind him.

He caught sight of her a few seconds later and quickly straightened, patted down his rumpled shirt, and replaced the look on his face with a more confident one. "There's nothing to worry about!"

That confident look was greatly undermined by the fit of coughing immediately following his declaration.

"Then why can't we breathe?" Ariel gasped, as his fit subsided.

Still panting, Captain Bud replied, "Give it time." He paused to catch his breath. "The circulation system... shut down last night...'s ok...got it going again."

"How?"

"I had to poke some holes in the filter."

With a mixture of bemusement (itself composed of equal parts oxygen deprivation and a morbid enjoyment of his obvious discomfort) and horror, Ariel replied, "And that helped?"

"It got the air moving." He took a deep breath and moved towards the kitchen.

"Why not just take the filter out?"

"Won't run if it's out." He stepped into the kitchen.

Ariel followed, concerned and annoyed in equal parts. "And we're okay?"

She found Captain Bud at the sink filling a cup with water, which he then chugged. With a sigh of relief, he put the cup down on the counter. It caught the raised edge of the sink and toppled over.

Paying no attention to the cup, which rolled all the way to the cold-wall side of the counter where it bounced onto the floor, he turned back to her. "Just like before, the air is better already."

As his statement did nothing to lessen her obvious disapproval, he elaborated. "Just with the doors closed the rooms are sealed, so we started running out of air."

"Ah," Ariel agreed darkly, "at least we're no more screwed than we were."

Captain Bud grudgingly acknowledged her point with a nod before continuing. "We're only a day out from the zone. Our SOS should be picked up by one of the border buoys any time now."

Ariel's disbelief was as palpable as the air. "Are you sure the transmitter actually works?"

"Of course it does," he said defensively, then grumbled to himself, "the inspectors *always* check that."

CHAPTER TWENTY-TWO

"PCV *Hamilton*, this is Ginhard System Control," a gruff voice announced. "We have received your identification, and you are ordered to hold position until the portmaster grants your clearance."

"Acknowledged, Control," Dianne Hamilton responded. "Holding position."

"Do you think it will take long?" Violette asked from "her station" on the starboard side of the bridge.

"No idea," her mother replied. "Normally clearance is just a rubber stamp, but we're unscheduled and, with everything that's going on, I imagine that they're triple checking everything."

"There's something going on?" Violette asked, feigning ignorance.

Dianne rolled her eyes, and Eric shushed his daughter from his seat on the opposite side of the bridge.

"*Hamilton*, your clearance is granted," the gruff voice declared after a long silence. "The scout boat *Sutton* will escort you to a docking orbit."

"Acknowledged, Control." Dianne's voice raised slightly, betraying her concern. She muted the channel and said, "A municipal escort? They've *really* increased security!"

"Maybe they just know about your criminal past!" Violette suggested.

"Or yours," Eric responded.

"GSB *Sutton* to PCV *Hamilton*," a new voice said.

Dianne shushed them both, then unmuted the channel. "Acknowledged, *Sutton*, this is *Hamilton*."

"*Hamilton*, we will be handling navigation, please lock onto our signal."

"Acknowledged, *Sutton*." Dianne tapped a few controls. "Follow mode engaged. You have the helm."

"Confirmed, *Hamilton*." The voice paused, then continued in a friendlier tone. "Don't worry, this is just the new routine. We'll have you planet-side in a few hours."

"Acknowledged, *Sutton*," Dianne said, relaxing. "We're grateful and anxious to make port."

As promised, a few hours later, they were in high orbit above the planet Ginhard and docked with an inspection station.

A middle-aged individual in grey coveralls stepped out of the port docking arm carrying a large bag over one shoulder. A moment later, five workers in blue coveralls followed.

The individual in grey shifted the bag to position it behind his back, smiled, then extended his hand.

"I'm Inspector Georges Carême, and my team will be handling your entry inspection today."

"Captain Dianne Hamilton." She took his hand. After releasing it, she said, "And this is my husband Eric."

Eric and the inspector shook hands briefly, then the inspector reached back to pull a large screen out of his bag.

"We should probably start the cargo inspection right away so we don't keep you here any longer than necessary," he said, gesturing to his crew.

"We always appreciate the efficiency of our inspections at this end." Dianne smiled and nodded to Eric. "My husband will show your crew to the cargo container, and I'll escort you through our vessel."

Four of the workers in blue followed Eric through the storeroom and on to the cargo hold elevator located across the main corridor from the foyer.

"Before we start, and off-the-record," Carême said slyly, his remaining assistant turning away purposefully as he pulled a small package from his bag, "my husband made me promise to give these to you when he heard you were out of Prosperity." He handed the package over. "It's not much, but they're widely regarded as the best snicker-doodles on the station."

"That's very kind," Dianne replied sincerely, slipping them into the large pocket on the front of her overalls.

Inspector Carême cleared his throat, and his remaining assistant stepped up beside him, her face clearly being forced into a serious expression.

"We'll start with a few quick scans," he said, waving his assistant through the door.

After the inspection was complete, Inspector Carême sent his crew back to the station and, after the last one disappeared down the docking arm, his expression darkened.

"Everything checks out but," he said with discomfort, "unfortunately, there has been a development since I came on board that I am obliged to make you aware of."

"What," Dianne asked with trepidation.

"This morning, the SDA declared the Prosperity Zone a loss," he replied flatly.

"Well, we knew that," Dianne said, with relief in her voice. "The station was destroyed."

"Yes," he said, shifting his weight and glancing down at his screen, "that was the physical loss. This is an *administrative* loss."

Dianne closed her eyes. "I don't think I like where this is going."

"I don't either." He stuffed his screen into his bag. "But I'm in the unenviable position of having to deliver the bad news."

"Go ahead," she replied, opening her eyes and looking at the inspector with resignation.

"Due to the loss of Prosperity Station and the Prosperity Corporate Zone administration complex located thereon," he said formally, "Prosperity ship registrations are no longer valid. There will be a grace period for vessels in transit until they complete their currently logged voyage, but a new registration will be required before they can leave port again."

"Frag," she said under her breath, then louder, "we were just planning to stay long enough to resupply and don't even have enough to cover that. I don't see how we can afford a new registration until we get paid for our cargo."

"Yeah, that's about what I expected," Inspector Carême replied, with a pained expression. "I wish there was something I could do beyond referring you to the local shipping office."

They shook hands a final time, and he quietly stepped back into the docking arm.

Once the *Hamilton* was settled into a parking orbit, Dianne took the shuttle down to Flanders, the capital city of Ginhard. It was early in the morning when she arrived, and most of the transient population hadn't stepped through their Doors yet, so it was nearly silent.

The Ginhard Spacecraft Registry Office was in the industrial district, a series of small offices each containing just a receptionist and a Door. After being cleared by the receptionist, Dianne stepped through the Door and onto the shipping guild station in geosynchronous orbit over Ginhard's largest continent located on the opposite side of the planet.

The office was plain but functional and well kept. Each window was fed by a zig-zagging waiting line marked by rope barriers. Dianne got into the line that led to the window labeled "Registrations."

"I'm a captain out of Prosperity Station," she said, when her turn at the window finally arrived. "I understand that my current registration is no longer valid and need to find out what I need to do."

Charles Pendleton, as identified by a digital name tag, repeated her question to the screen in front of him, nodded, then replied, "You will need to file for a local registration."

"Okay, let's do that."

"What is your ship registry?"

"PCV *Hamilton*."

Pendleton repeated the registration to the screen, then said, "I see it. Any changes to the configuration?"

"No, no changes."

"Good, that will speed things along. I'll need your account information for the fee."

Dianne shifted uncomfortably. "About that. Our main accounts were with a Prosperity Station bank."

"That's unfortunate. Do you have an alternative means of payment?"

"All we have left is our guild account, and we need that for food. I was under the impression that the emergency provisions covered issues like this."

"I'm sorry, but there's nothing in the assistance package about ship registrations and, *by law,* we can't start your registration application until we receive the fee, *in full.* You will need to find an alternative means of payment before your grace period ends, which is thirty days after you arrived in the system."

"What if we can't pay the fee before then?"

"That's not my department, but usually unregistered vessels are subject to daily fines until the lapsed registration is renewed, the vessel is scrapped, or changes hands."

"*Daily* fines? If we can't pay the registration fee, how are we expected to pay the fines?"

"Most people pay them out of what they get for selling the unregistered vessel."

"We can't sell *our home!*"

"I'm sorry," Pendleton said, without conviction, "but I can't change the rules."

"Are you sure that there isn't something we can do?" Dianne asked in frustration. "Considering the circumstances, can't we work out some kind of deferral or payment plan?"

"I'm afraid not." He shook his head, then continued with a bored look. "As I said, we cannot begin the registration process until the fee has been paid in full. I recommend that you visit the public assistance office. I hear they're handing out payments to people in your situation. Perhaps that will resolve your issue." He dismissed her with his eyes, then looked past her. "Next in line please."

Exiting back through the same Door from which she'd arrived, Dianne proceeded to trek to the opposite side of Flanders and into Government Center, where the Public Assistance Office was located.

The Public Assistance Office was bustling. Dozens of reps worked through the long sorting line one by one until it was Dianne's turn.

"I'm a captain out of Prosperity Station. I've been informed that my registration is no longer valid, but our bank was on Prosperity so we can't pay the fee."

"Please head over to line F. They will be able to assist you."

The wait at line F was much shorter, and soon Dianne found herself at the window talking with Charlene Guiteau, according to her name tag, a woman her own age. She repeated her issue.

"I'm sure we can help you out. Can you provide your ID?"

Dianne passed her wristband over a disk embedded in the counter.

"I have some bad news," Guiteau said, frowning at her screen. "According to our logs, you have already received your entitlement—a supply drop delivered by the ΔPS *Steadfast.*"

"I'm not worried about the money, just making sure that my family still has a place to live."

"The legislation was very strict on this point. Each family unit was allocated one supply drop or one stimulus payment."

"But we're stuck here with no income until we can sell our cargo, but with Prosperity gone, there's no one to sell it to. If we don't register our ship, which we can't afford to do without selling our cargo, we're going to start getting fined."

"But you *did* receive the supply drop."

"Yes, but it's nearly gone now."

"I understand your situation, and I sympathize, but my hands are tied. If your daughter was a few years older we could probably manage a payment for her, but as it is—"

"So, what do we do?" Dianne interrupted in frustration.

"There are charities that are helping people in your situation," Guiteau started weakly, then brightened. "Wait, I think I can put in a request under the relief articles of the assistance legislation that would defer your registration fee until you sell your cargo but still begin the registration process immediately." She tapped at her screen to call up the relevant text.

"I've already been to the registration office. They told me that there wasn't anything covering registrations in the assistance package."

"Yeah, sorry about that," she said absently, while she tapped at her screen. "Technically, they're correct. The package was not designed to cover registration renewals. However, there is an associated expenses section, which was written to be quite broad so that it would cover general costs directly resulting from the incident. Everyone is still scrambling to figure out how to handle the disincorporation of the PCZ. The registration office probably hasn't had to deal with this situation yet."

"Yeah, join the club."

"Here it is!" Guiteau exclaimed, finding the clause she was looking for. After scanning it for a moment she smiled. "With this, I'm sure that I could have your temporary papers in a few days. Perhaps then you could do some deliveries to make ends meet?"

"The only things that ship by vessel are ZPGs, Portals, and Doors; everything else can just go through a Portal. There are no factories on Ginhard, and *we* have the only supply of Doors in the system. Even if we could find something to haul, where would we put it? We can't leave our current cargo unattended or we lose the salvage rights."

"I wish I had something better to offer."

Dianne sighed. "I'm sorry. I'm letting my frustration with the whole situation get to me. You've actually been extremely helpful. If you can get the registration moving that would at least keep us from having to not pay the fines."

CHAPTER TWENTY-THREE

Lieutenant Diogo de Abreu, the VPS *Audace*'s communications officer on duty, reported from his station at the front of the bridge. "Captain, I'm receiving an SOS from an incoming craft reporting life support failure."

"Do we have identification?" Captain Brugnaro replied.

"Confirming now. PLV... oh, you've *got* to be kidding..." Lieutenant de Abreu caught himself and said, "Sorry, sir. The vessel is identified as the PLV *Rockhard*."

"That's quite..." Captain Brugnaro started then shook his head. "No, I'm not even going to comment."

"I have tracking on the *Rockhard*," Lieutenant Jamie Cooke, the detection officer on duty, said with a bemused look. "At current velocity, the vessel will enter zone space in fifty-two minutes."

Captain Brugnaro toggled a switch on the control panel in front of him. "Flight control, dispatch a recovery flight to intercept a vessel in distress, full life support failure protocols, detection will provide coordinates. Communications, see if you can raise the vessel's captain."

"I'm signaling, but there's no response," Lieutenant de Abreu reported, with a shake of his head.

The *Rockhard*'s docking hatch swung open to admit the six members of the *Steadfast*'s recovery team. Each member of the team was wearing a tight-fitting red environmental suit with attached bowl helmet and a crowded utility belt.

"SOS listed two on board," Lieutenant Dorina Amundsen said formally. "Standard search protocol."

The team moved efficiently towards the front of the ship, one stepping into the bathroom to push aside the shower curtain while the other five headed into the open living area.

"One unresponsive physically male individual here," Ensign Kit Bailey reported, as they kneeled down in front of the couch and quickly pulled a small device from their belt. "Applying respirator. Medical ID indicates that this is Captain Lawrence Nesmith, 26 years of age, no underlying conditions."

"Prakash, help Bailey get the captain into the shuttle. Bao, check the room across the corridor."

"The room's locked," Ensign Bao Dazhu said. "I need the Pic."

Lieutenant Amundsen pulled a small red block out of a large pouch on his belt and handed it to Bao, who took it and placed it over the Pad next to the door. A yellow light appeared on the top of the block, which flashed for a moment before turning green. Ensign Bao shifted his grip to just the upper half of the block and twisted clockwise. The top half spun along a barely visible seam, making a soft clicking sound at regular intervals as it turned. When the upper half completed 90 degrees of rotation, there was a dull crunching noise from beneath the Pic. After a moment, the Pic chirped, and the door slid open.

"The other one is in here!" Bao said, moving into the room. "Unresponsive physically female individual. Applying respirator. Medical ID indicates that she is Ariel Anthony, 24 years of age, no underlying conditions."

"Get her to the shuttle. I'll report back to flight control."

Captain Bud was in agony. His chest felt heavy, and his breath was a painful rattle as it scraped its way through his raw throat. There was a clinging pressure on his face. He tried to brush the object aside, but it hung on tightly.

A second attempt to dislodge it also failed, and the flexible thing responded by aggressively leaping back onto his face. With a burst of terror, he realized that he was being attacked by a soft wheezing creature that had clamped itself around his head. He started to rise from his prone position to make a third attempt.

"Woah there," the creature said, as something large pressed down on him. "Stay still."

Captain Bud fought valiantly but was unable to free himself. He must have been making some progress, however, because the creature shouted for help. "Doctor!"

"Mr. Nesmith," a female voice said, "calm down and open your eyes."

So caught up in the battle with the creature, Captain Bud had forgotten to conduct a visual inspection of the situation. Slightly embarrassed by the oversight, he complied.

Past the translucent creature on his face, which he could now see had a long, curving tail, he could just make out two blurry humanoid shapes: one yellow and the other white.

"You're going to be okay," the more distant white shape said reassuringly, with the female voice.

Captain Bud's vision slowly came into focus, and he saw that the white shape was an older, passably attractive, woman wearing a lab coat. The yellow shape, still pressing him down into what he could now identify as a narrow utilitarian bed, was clearly a person in head-to-toe medical garb. The wheezing creature on his face, he finally realized, was just an oxygen mask. Captain Bud stopped struggling.

"Can I let go of you now?" the yellow shape asked.

Captain Bud nodded his head weakly and the shape stood back—but didn't move far from the edge of the bed.

"You've been through an ordeal," the woman in white said. "You need to rest for a little while."

Captain Bud nodded in agreement, settled back, and took her advice.

He awoke again several hours later and was able to make a more detailed inspection of his surroundings.

To his right, and attached to the wall, was a large equipment cabinet with several screens, Pads, and drawers installed in the front of it. He could just make out his full legal name on the screen closest to his head. The room was filled with seven other beds, all identical to his and all empty except for the one immediately to his left. His companion from the *Rockhard* was there, breathing roughly under her own oxygen mask.

Even covered by a rough blanket, her hair mussed and bunched up beneath the mask's strap, she was a pleasant sight. He smiled to himself, and groggily thought that perhaps now that they were free of their confinement, she might finally go back to the person he had hit it off so well with at the Linner party.

Captain Bud watched her on and off for over an hour before she started to stir. He rose up on his elbow as her eyes fluttered open, darted around the room in panic, then finally slowed and focused on his face.

He smiled. "Hey, beautiful."

Her eyes widened, and she nearly threw herself off the bed.

"Get away from me!" she shouted, fumbling at her mask. "I never want to see your cheap face again!"

"C'mon…" Captain Bud started, as a yellow shape rushed towards them.

Ariel freed herself from the mask just as the yellow shape arrived.

"Frag no!" she shouted, while the yellow shape tried to press her back down onto the bed. As she struggled, she glared at Captain Bud with pure hate in her eyes. "I swear, if I had a time machine right now, I wouldn't go back and kill baby Hitler, *I'd kill you!*"

CHAPTER TWENTY-FOUR

"I'll be there at 10AM sharp," Dianne Hamilton said to the face hovering beside her wrist, then she tapped the **DISCONNECT** button projected on her forearm.

After the face disappeared, she broke into a large grin and shouted, "Finally!"

"Did it sell?!" Violette asked, rushing into her mother's office, her father following close behind.

"They signed the papers about an hour ago. That was the new director of operations. We're finally going to be able to offload!" She paused. "After some negotiations, of course."

"It's been *months!*" Violette said. "Just give them whatever they want! I'm so tired of this *untextured* food!"

"Absolutely not," her mother replied firmly. "We're sitting on the *only* supply of new Doors in the system. I'm *not* going to just give them away."

The former Prosperity office was in a state of disarray when Dianne arrived there the next morning. It had been ransacked when the original staff had been terminated via bulk notification, and only the essentials had been replaced, most of which were still in boxes stacked in the back left-hand corner.

The receptionist was sitting at a simple and roughly-printed table equipped with only a single large portable screen, which was propped up by a kickstand built into its back.

"I'm scheduled to meet with Hadrian Rothschild at 10," Dianne said politely.

"Captain Hamilton, yes. Please take a…" the receptionist paused and looked around the room. "Sorry, just give me a moment."

He stood and went over to the back corner, then moved a box off a chair that was just as rough as his table. He carried it to the front of the room and placed it near the large picture window.

"Sorry," he said, as he wiped the seat off with his sleeve. "First day. We haven't even figured out a decor yet, let alone furniture. Mr. Rothschild will be with you shortly."

Dianne was escorted into Rothschild's office over an hour later. Like the lobby, his office was a shambles populated by an identical temporary table, some more rough chairs, and a small stack of boxes.

"I've been authorized to reinstate your contract and immediately take delivery of the product," he said, after the pleasantries had been completed.

"Hold on, our contract was terminated. That gives us certain rights."

"Yes, but we know you've been stuck in orbit for several months and don't want to prolong the process any more than necessary. I'm sure the wait has been difficult for you and your family. Reinstating the existing contract is the quickest and easiest solution."

"Except that Door sets are selling for more than three times what they were before the incident."

"True," Rothschild said with a small smile, "but, as we both know, only authorized agents can sell them."

"Agreed," Dianne said, smiling back, "but authorized agents can't sell Doors they don't have."

"Fair point, but your shipment is not the only one on its way from the station…" A look of discomfort crossed his face. "Sorry, the former site of Prosperity station."

"I'm pretty sure you're wrong about that." Dianne overlooked the still painful reference and pressed her point. "The *Faro*'s shipment was claimed by the Navy, and we both know it will end up in a far more influential sector. And I've known the captain of the *Shin* for years, and I'm certain that he headed off to greener pastures the instant Prosperity terminated their contract."

"You're certainly entitled to your opinion, but I'm confident we can source what we need."

"Okay, fine. Let's look for a middle ground. I'm willing to take 50% of the current retail price, and we'll drop off the container wherever you want it."

"Your original delivery fee would have been a tiny fraction of that," he said, with a disapproving look. "We'd be taking a heavy loss if we agreed to that proposal. Besides, we're only interested in the cargo at this time. I can offer you the original wholesale cost of the Doors."

"Retaining the shipping container will incur storage or disposal costs. I'll need at least twice original retail just to break even."

"That's an exaggeration, even considering the costs of being stuck in-system for so long, you'd still be making a huge profit at our expense. I can offer original retail price but, that's really cutting our margin to the quick."

"Now, *you're* exaggerating. With Prosperity Station gone, we had to re-register the *Hamilton*, and we'll need to pay docking and inspection fees before we can even start offloading. I'll go to one and three quarters original retail, but that would be cutting *our* margin to the quick."

"I might be able to manage one and a half retail and have a 5% initial payment in your account by the end of the day to cover your fees, if you can meet a few conditions."

"Depends on the conditions." Dianne paused for a moment and, remembering Violette's distraction during the trip, quickly added a condition of her own. "Oh, I almost forgot, we need to keep two of the deluxe sets so we can get reconnected."

"Fine," Rothschild replied, making a note on the portable screen propped on the desk between them.

Dianne was caught by surprise, having expected a haggle down to just the open set of Doors, but quickly recovered. "And your conditions?"

"First, we'd like to ship a quarter of those Doors to the Abioye company on Tunis as repayment for a loan that helped us buy this office. It would be at standard delivery contract rates."

"Okay," she said, as he hesitated, "and…"

He made a show of examining his screen, then said, "We weren't able to purchase all of the old Prosperity warehouse space, so we'll need you to pick up your original return delivery."

"And deliver it to?"

"Well," Rothschild shifted in his chair, "we thought that we could set up a storage contract."

"We're not registered for storage. No cargo vessel is. The shipping guild would never allow it," Dianne said, an idea forming in her mind. "Guild rules prohibit carrying any off-contract cargo that doesn't belong to us."

"Perhaps we could contract you to deliver it back to us after the Tunis drop-off," Rothschild attempted.

"Now you're just baiting me. The guild would never approve a contract shipping to the departure port."

"Perhaps we could work out a purchase deal?" Rothschild suggested hopefully.

"Purchase?!" Dianne said, maintaining a disgusted look despite the feeling of victory washing over her. "What do you expect us to do with a hold full of broken doors?"

"What if we increase the purchase price of your current cargo by 1% to offset the cost." At Dianne's unconvinced look, Rothschild quickly added, "And we'll cover all docking and loading fees for both delivery and pickup."

"That's very generous." Dianne leaned back in her chair and smiled predatorily. "I'm betting that you don't have the space for our load of Doors without the pickup."

Rothschild maintained a neutral expression and did not reply.

"Fine, I'm a team player," Dianne said, in a consoling tone, "but I want a disposal contract for the pickup, standard rates and conditions."

"Deal," Rothschild agreed quickly, looking both relieved and uncomfortable. "I'll have the contracts drawn up and forwarded to the guild for approval immediately."

"So, we're stuck with the container *and* a load of broken Doors?" Eric asked, after his wife summarized the deal.

"Relax, it's not so bad," Dianne replied confidently. "Remember, I was a Door and Portal technician for twenty years before I got promoted. Even without spare parts I will probably be able to get most of them working, and since they're part of a disposal contract, we have full rights to sell them in any condition, *including fully operational*, without going through an agent."

Eric did not look convinced. "Are you sure? We're almost through this. I don't want to get stuck with a bunch of scrap that we have to pay to get rid of."

Dianne smiled reassuringly. "Even if we did have to scrap the whole load, we did *very* well on this deal. The salvage laws were written with the presumption that there would be little to no price fluctuation for the cargo. Giving us salvage rights was only intended to cover operating costs and delay losses. With the current Door market, we made a *very* nice profit." She laughed. "I would have been thrilled with original retail."

"And you're sure?"

"I am. In fact, I did a spot check while they were loading." She pulled up an inventory on her screen, the margins were filled with her personal notes. "Here, see? This one only needs a new backup battery. I'm sure that I can get one from a nearly new Door I saw with a damaged frame. And this one just has a system passcode that the previous owner never turned off. I can swap out the control boards with boards from some of the un-matched endpoints. I'm also going to reach out to some of my contacts from the old days to see if anyone saved some system images locally. If I can find the right one, I could fix that control board, too."

She stuffed her screen into the front pocket of her overalls and smiled widely. "And that's just the start. They were so desperate to empty that warehouse that they just loaded *everything*. I didn't want to look too close during transfer and tip my hand, but I saw quite a few Doors that didn't have inspection tags. I'm sure some of those were from upgrades and are probably in perfect working order. I can do this!"

"If you're good with it then so am I," Eric said with relief. "I was just worried that we'd get stuck with a lot of junk."

"Well," Dianne replied with a smirk, "there *is* an Archer set in there. They barely got those things to market before the reliability lawsuits started pouring in."

"There's always one bad apple I guess." He grinned. "So, what's the next step?"

"I meet with their rep on Tunis next week. Since Abioye is an investor and a former Prosperity site, they're letting me use their site-to-site Door."

"Wow." Eric stepped back and gave her an exaggerated apprising look. "Another in-person meeting! You're moving up in the world!"

"Yeah, sure," she replied with a laugh, "except that it's just a new company anxious to confirm the delivery details so that they don't have to be bothered with it later. But now," she said, pulling a data chip in a clear case from her pocket and holding it up, "I've got something to do."

Dianne took the chip to the bridge but didn't stay very long. When she returned, she went directly to the family room, where her daughter and husband were waiting. With a bright smile on her face, she announced, "Now that all the fees are paid, I was able to update our temporary registration. We are now *officially* aboard the *Ginhard* Cargo Vessel *Hamilton*."

EPILOGUE

Dianne Hamilton was met at the Door by a tall, heavy-set woman her own age in a smart business suit—a subtle wave pattern was flowing gently through the dark blue fabric.

"Captain Dianne Hamilton, I presume," the woman said with a smile.

"I am," Dianne replied. "But I'm afraid that they didn't tell me who I was meeting with to finalize my delivery contract."

"That's my fault," the woman replied, with a bemused expression. "I'm Nala Abioye, CEO of Abioye, Inc."

"It's a pleasure to meet you, Ms. Abioye," Dianne said, slightly taken aback. "Are you still staffing up?"

"Not really, and call me Nala." She gestured towards a suite behind the empty reception desk that contained three small, apparently unoccupied, offices. "As you may know, this used to be a Prosperity support coordination site, so it's a pretty confined space."

"Yes," Dianne said, nodding, "several of my technicians worked through here."

"Oh, good," Nala replied, directing her into the largest office. "Did your work ever bring you here?"

"No," Dianne said, stepping in and standing in front of the empty desk. "I was mainly management towards the end, didn't get out all that much."

"Of course," Nala replied, taking a seat and gesturing with one hand for Dianne to do the same.

As Dianne sat down, Nala rested her hand on the opposite sleeve of her suit and a series of waves traveled away from her hand in response.

"If we didn't already have an established company here on Tunis, we couldn't have really done much with this space," Nala said. "We acquired it for the workroom and tools."

"Do you run a service firm?"

"We're putting one together." Nala smiled. "I understand that you have some repair experience."

"Of course," Dianne said, folding her hands in her lap. "You need at least ten years in the field before you can be promoted above supervisor."

"Not something you'd forget, I imagine."

"No," Dianne laughed, "twenty-three years in the field leaves a permanent mark." She thought of the Doors in the *Hamilton*'s cargo hold. "But, it comes in handy now and again."

"I'm certain it does," Nala said, her smile widening. "In fact, I had been thinking that it might also come in handy for me."

"It's starting to sound like we're talking about more than a delivery contract."

"We are." Nala leaned forward. "There are no Door or Portal technicians on Tunis. The population has always been so low that none of the corporations saw fit to establish offices here, just pass-through locations like this one."

"But you want to change that."

"I do. I grew up here, founded my company here. Now, with Prosperity gone, I see a new *opportunity* here." She paused and leaned back in her chair; it creaked in response. "I'm going to need to train some technicians to become the core of my new venture."

"And you want me to teach them?"

"Not *just* teach," Nala said, leaning forward again, accompanied by another creak. "I want you to be the Director of Service Operations for Abioye's new Portal division." She paused again and spread her arms to indicate the facility around them. "We'll start here, train half a dozen techs, then have those techs train the next cohort, and so on. And eventually, I want *you* to be the one running the entire division."

Dianne was flattered but uncertain. "This really isn't what I was expecting."

"Life rarely is. I only glanced at your work history packet out of curiosity, but I'm glad I did. I have been struggling to find the right partner and had started to worry that this opportunity might slip by." Nala paused for a moment, then spread her arms. "But the universe provides." She pointed at Dianne. "I believe that *you* are the partner that I need. If we move forward together, and if everything proceeds as I expect it to, in a few years we can talk about capitalizing the P in partner and turning your work-equity into an ownership stake."

"It's a lot to take in," Dianne said, with an uneasy smile.

"But?"

"But, I think I need some time to let it sink in," Dianne said. "My family has been through a lot lately, and I'd like to discuss it with them before making a decision."

"I understand," Nala replied. "You'll have the offer packet before you get to the other side of the Door. Don't keep me waiting."

Despite repeated attempts by the best attorney that his family's money could buy, there had been no dissuading Captain Bud's former companion from filing her completely unfounded complaint. Even worse, somehow, she had convinced the judge not to dismiss the baseless charges, landing them both in court.

Now, uncomfortable in a very expensive suit, he watched with panic as the judge returned from his deliberations.

"C'mon, Annie," Captain Bud cried in desperation, "please *be reasonable.*"

Ariel sneered but the judge responded first. "You are to address the court, not the plaintiff!"

"But this is all so unfair!" Captain Bud whined in protest.

"The plaintiff has testified to two attempted sexual assaults—one preempted and the second requiring physical defense." He sat behind the bench. "You did not deny either incident. Are you attempting to change your testimony?"

"No, I'm not *changing* anything," Captain Bud continued with exasperation. "As I *already said*, those were just *misunderstandings...*"

"I didn't *misunderstand* anything," Ariel clarified with enmity.

"*Please*, be *reasonable*," Captain Bud said again. "This is all too much! I've already got inspectors nickel-and-diming me over all the new regulations…"

"Are *you* claiming financial hardship?" The judge gave him an annoyed look.

"Well, no." Captain Bud shifted uncomfortably as he unconsciously ran his hands down the smooth, hand-stitched fabric of his pant-legs. "Of course not."

"Then you are sentenced to five years of penal service per charge," the judge banged his gavel, "to begin immediately."

Captain Bud's heart sank at the pure injustice of it all. Why couldn't anyone listen to *his* side for a change?

As the bailiff took hold of his arm, he suddenly realized that it was going to take a *very* good plan to put the chill back this time.

"Are you *sure* about this?" Eric Hamilton asked, swiping through the contract.

"Absolutely not," his wife replied, "but, after everything that happened, I feel the need to be *anchored*. An opportunity this perfect may never come again."

"It's just so isolated…" Eric paused at his wife's incredulous look. "Not like *that!*" He paused again. "We'd have to *drive* to get anywhere!"

"Then we'll pick up a little Location in one of the city Collections, too," she replied. "I'm sure there's enough room in the house to install a second mount for that second set of deluxe Doors that I got out of our delivery."

"I suppose it could be a good investment with the way property prices are going," Eric replied, then laughed. "Who would have imagined that owning *dirt* could be an *investment*? We're back in the dark ages!"

Dianne smiled in response. "Just sign, dirt-owner."

A few hours later, a bright yellow automated Ulyft shuttle deposited the Hamilton family, and the endpoint of their slightly used deluxe Door set, on the landing pad in front of a large country-style house with a wraparound porch. A narrow driveway extended from the landing pad and eventually connected to an infrequently utilized street that connected to another, which finally connected to a busier avenue.

The farmhouse and acres of surrounding land had belonged to a local farmer until her passing the year previous. She had left neither heir nor will, so the property had landed in probate court and the farmland had gone to seed as the estate slowly made its way through the system. It had finally cleared the last hurdle not long after the Hamilton family's Door windfall.

As her parents leaned the tightly-wrapped Door against the porch railing beside the steps and the shuttle lifted off for its next pickup, Violette ran out to the center of the landing pad and started spinning with her arms stretched out. "I can't believe this is all ours!"

Later, after their daughter had fallen asleep in her new "planet-room," Eric and Dianne sat together on a bench built into the inner wall of the porch.

"Violette wants to stay here forever," Eric said to his wife, smiling as he remembered his daughter's unconstrained joy.

"Would that be so bad? I like the idea of Violette putting down roots here."

Eric lifted his head from his wife's shoulder. "But what about the *Hamilton*? I figured we would be splitting our time between here and there, maybe hiring a relief captain to pick up the slack. After all, your family has been running cargo on it for generations."

"Oh, I'd never get rid of the *Hamilton*!" Dianne laughed. "My dad would come back and haunt me for the rest of my life if I even *thought* about selling it. I'm pretty sure that I could get assigned to a route between here and Tunis or one of the other local systems."

"Wouldn't it be hard?" Eric said, with concern in his voice. "Even with a relief captain you'd be away quite a bit."

"Maybe not, there's talk about changing the laws to allow automated vessels…"

"Seriously?" Eric said in surprise. "They haven't allowed automated spaceships of any kind since the First Wave!"

"Seriously, we've always known that it's an outdated law, but it wasn't worth anyone's effort to change before the incident. The first PCV *Hamilton* was running itself long before Grandpa bought this one. We've been little more than legally-mandated supervisors for centuries."

"I suppose that's true." Eric grinned. "Everyone knows that all captains do is tap a screen every few days."

Dianne punched him playfully in the shoulder. "We'd still need someone to be on standby for emergencies and to be physically onboard during docking procedures and, of course, to perform critical screen tapping duties."

Still grinning, Eric asked, "So are you saying that we're full-time planet-siders now?"

"I guess I am."

"Wow, I was still getting used to the idea of part-time. It's going to be quite an adjustment."

"It will. Despite everything, I want to keep one foot in space." Dianne gazed out at the starry night sky with a smile. "But mainly I plan on spending as much time as possible puttering around this new anchor of ours."

About the Author

Daniel J. Lyons grew up along the east coast of the U.S. as a Navy brat before settling in Massachusetts. He started writing fan fiction in high school, then earned a degree in journalism with a minor in creative writing before unexpectedly focusing on a career as an IT professional, eventually specializing in web and mobile communication. *Severed*, his first novel, was written in 2020 both as therapy for and as a reaction to sheltering in place during the COVID-19 pandemic.

Other Works by Daniel J. Lyons

The Infinitesimal Collection: Bureaucracy, Stuffed Bears and Alien Duels

A short story collection including:

- "A Visit to the Licensing Department"
  A science fiction story about what life might be like if human lives were cheapened to the point where they could be taken legally as long as you have the correct permit.

- "The Busiest Workday"
  A speculative fiction story told by a mid-level angel that attempts to answer the question "will bureaucracy ever end?" by documenting the heavenly aftermath of the apocalypse.

- "Come Around Here Often?"
  A science fiction story told by Captain Wilson Banski who, after an enemy attack destroys his ship, deals with misadventure and cultural misunderstandings after his escape pod lands on an alien planet.

- "Best Friend Bears"
  A fiction piece told by Sarah about growing up with her best friend Ann and their special pair of stuffed bears.

Visit *DansFormers.info* for a full bibliography.

CPSIA information can be obtained
at www.ICGtesting.com
Printed in the USA
BVHW032135271120
594405BV00012B/52/J